Once Upon a Time Long, Long Ago

Henry Shykoff

Illustrated by Marilyn Mets

Once Upon A Time: Long, Long Ago
Henry Shykoff

Published by Natural Heritage/Natural History Inc.
P.O. Box 95, Station O, Toronto, Ontario M4A 2M8

Canadian Cataloguing in Publication Data

Shykoff, Henry
    Once upon a time, long, long ago

ISBN 1-896219-58-6

1. Prehistoric peoples — Juvenile fiction. I. Mets, Marilyn. II. Title.

PS8587.H94O52 1999   jC813'54   C99-931737-7
PZ7.S5624On 1999

Cover, illustrations and text design by Marilyn Mets & Peter Ledwon, Blue Sky Studio, Toronto
Edited by Jane Gibson
Printed and bound in Canada by Hignell Printing Limited, Winnipeg, Manitoba.

Natural Heritage/Natural History Inc. acknowledges the support received for its publishing program from the Canada Council Block Grant Program. We also acknowledge with gratitude the assistance of the Association for the Export of Canadian Books, Ottawa.

For my grandchildren Michael and Sarah and Pierre
(and other children who like stories of this kind)

Introduction: Why Did I Do This?

Early one summer, my grandson Michael, then four and one half years old, asked me, "When did people start?" I began to tell him about "Lucy," the 3,000,000- year-old fossil remains, found by Donald Johanson, at that time the oldest known possible ancestor of mankind.

"No that's not what I want," he said. "When did people who look like us start?"

I told him that I did not know but believed that it was somewhere between 150,000 to 200,000 years ago. I told him that when I was young there were cave people stories to be found, which I had enjoyed. I would try to find some for him. Despite my best efforts not a one could I find. Seemingly it was up to me, so I decided to write a collection of short stories on this theme for Michael. I started, but Michael did not like what I had written.

"Too scary," he said.

I tried again, this time beginning with a more positive note, and developing the story as I had envisioned it. The characters I had created, however, did not follow the path I had chosen, but took over and told their own story.

By the time I had finished, Michael was almost six years old and was reading by himself. He liked my story. So did a number of children, some of whom were already readers, and some of whom were not yet ready to read but were avid listeners. The three girls next door, a set of twelve-year-old twins and their sister, a fourteen-year-old also, found my work of interest. It was suggested, by both children and adult friends, that I publish my story. So I did—a story for children of all ages.

Background: Where and When Did "Us" Begin?

This story of adventure and discovery, set in the period some 50,000 years ago, marks the beginning of a sudden, almost explosive alteration in people's behaviour. By then, people had existed for about 100,000 years. In appearance they were very much as we are today. Brain size was similar and so probably was intelligence, but without our accumulated life knowledge. About 50,000 years ago, people, for some reason, suddenly changed from being just another medium-sized mammal, one of a group of hominids, to being what we think of as "us." Tools were no longer merely "make-do" but became more complex, more specialized and actually beautiful. There was the beginning of art and the beginning of music. Communication between people greatly improved as language became more complex.

From then on people were what we term human. The essential difference between people then and now was that they lacked the five hundred centuries of shared living experience which they were just beginning to accumulate. This experience has been handed down to us, generation by generation, through their descendants, our ancestors.

What caused this change? Perhaps it was the development of language beyond more primitive sounds. Perhaps, as some think, it was a partnership with wolves which strengthened their hunting skills and allowed this group of hominids to become dominant. Perhaps there were some curious individuals who wanted to understand how things worked. All of these possible themes are used in this story, especially the last one; the effect that a few curious and reasoning people can have on their society.

Whatever the reason, it appears that Homo erectus,

Neanderthal or Homo sapiens, and any other hominids that may have coexisted, could not compete with our ancestors, the Cro-Magnon, the group also known as Homo sapiens sapiens or "modern man." The others are now extinct, leaving "us" as the only hominid survivors. Perhaps too, given Homo sapiens sapiens' tendency to eliminate rivals, we may have been the reason that Neanderthal man became extinct. Our record of respect for life is not good, seemingly from the earliest of times.

The sequence of events in this story fits what little is known about that time. There is little fossil record of Cro-Magnon man and only slightly more fossil record of the Neanderthal. We do know that for about 50,000 years Neanderthal and Cro-Magnon coexisted, but inexplicably Neanderthal disappeared about 35,000 years ago. There have been some fossils discovered that might be those of a mixture of the two species, the latest occurring in Portugal in December 1998, when the fossil of a four-year-old child with features of both Neanderthal and Cro-Magnon, was found. Despite these findings, it seems that there are no "Homo sapiens neanderthalensis" among us. At the time of this writing, no DNA study results on this most recent discovery have been published.

It would appear that we are the only hominids alive. In the time period of our story, that would not have been true. Fossil records show that Cro-Magnon and Neanderthal lived side by side in close proximity for many millennia, but in this story we meet only our species, Homo sapiens sapiens (wise, wise man) and experience with them the dawning of humanity as we know it.

Geographically, the setting is the area approximately where Syria, Lebanon and Israel come together. The world was well into the last ice age and the great glacier was spreading over much of Europe, Asia and North America, encroaching steadily southward. The climate probably would have been similar to that found today in southern and central Ontario and the northeastern United States. It was to become much colder over the following 30,000 years.

The animals were those of cooler temperate climates. It was too warm as yet for the woolly mammoth, but all members of the deer family, from the largest, the elk, to small gazelles, were found. Horses, too, were becoming plentiful. They had originated in North America, had crossed the Bering land bridge, and spread across Siberia, China and the steppes of the Ukraine. From there they moved into Europe, the near East and North Africa. Along with these grass eaters came all their predators, including the most ferocious of them all, the sabre-toothed tiger.

In the midst of these animals lived our ancestors, Homo sapiens, as represented by our characters in this story, two children ages 10 and 12 who, having become separated from their parents, are forced to be courageous and inventive in order to survive.

The story begins in the "home cave" which would be located about 60 km east of Mt. Hermon, a little east of the current Israel-Syria border, somewhat south and east of where the city of Damascus is now.

The clan cave of Mother would be near the headwaters of the Jordan River where the old shrines to the god Pan are found, the Banias.

Table of Contents

One

The Clan

The boy Sim sat watching the flickering light on the cave wall. He felt good. He was warm and dry. For the first time since the season of the berries he was not hungry. He was comfortable. This day was so different from what he had known! A great change had taken place over the past three days and he had a feeling of satisfaction and pride he had never felt before. His sister Eevo lay curled up sleeping nearby.

Five days ago everything had been horrible. The bad time started after Mother and Father had gone a long way off to find Mother's clan. Father's only knife, the flint one she had given him, had broken. In her clan there were people who knew how to make flint knives and scrapers, but no one in his clan had this skill. Without a knife, the skinning of animals after a hunt was extremely difficult, sometimes almost impossible. They had to go to Mother's people where a new knife could be made.

But Mother did not know how to find her home clan. She knew she had been lost and had wandered for four days before Father rescued her from the hyenas. She remembered that she had told him that they called themselves the "Wet-land Clan." But go they must! In preparation for the journey, she had gathered the best of the few skins she had cured, to trade for a knife and to give as gifts.

Ideally, they all would have gone together, Mother, Father, Eevo and Sim, but Sim could not walk very well. He had been born lame, born with a "club foot." Because of this, Sim and his sister Eevo stayed behind. Ab, Father's good friend and hunting partner, had promised to look after both of them, but especially Sim, since so many people of the clan resented the lame child. Early one morning, the rising sun behind them, the parents left.

Good food providers were important to the clan and Mother and Father were among the best. But now they were gone. Soon after their departure, both Ab and Ro, his hunting partner, had been attacked by a pack of hyenas, fierce dog-like animals, and badly injured. If they recovered they might be able to provide the clan with food again, but it would take many moons. Only two able hunters were left, Yo, an adult, and Og, an older boy who was now given the job of a man. The long cold time was coming and the people were afraid. Would there be enough food? Who would look after the lame boy? How could they feed people who could not help gather food? Everybody might be in danger of starving, especially if the winter was a harsh one. The crippled one only meant more work for someone. He was more trouble, they felt, than he was worth.

Sim was about 10 years old, taller than the other boys

his age and quite strong, but lame. He would never be a hunter and a food provider. In the eyes of the clan he was useless, and they called him Sim, meaning the "lame one." His sister, Eevo, about two years older and almost a woman, could work. The people saw her as useful and wanted her to stay.

At first, everything had gone on as before for Sim. But when as many days as there are fingers on a hand had passed, and Mother and Father had not returned, the people of the clan chased him away. Yelling and throwing stones at him, they drove him far away from the safety of the cave.

The people of this group or clan lived inside a large cave. At night they huddled together for warmth and protection. These early humans were really a group of medium-sized mammals, rather weak and slow compared to the other animals that lived around them. As hunters, they were not quite fast enough or strong enough to catch more than the occasional small animal for food. They ate what they could find, a diet of mice, insects or grubs and, if they could steal it, the remains of any larger beast that some stronger predator had killed. Whenever possible, plant roots were dug to eat and, in the hot season before the time of falling leaves, there were plenty of berries, a special treat for everyone. This was the only time of the year when the people were without hunger.

Not many people were living in the world at that time. The few people that did exist, lived in small family groups or clans. Each cave, usually found at some distance from another clan's cave, sheltered only twenty or thirty people. Since the surrounding land did not provide enough food for any more people, the size of each family group was small. Many babies died because there was not enough food for the mothers. Babies born in the winter season usually did not survive because there was no way to keep them warm. Any serious injury was almost always fatal. Under these harsh conditions, people might easily have become extinct and disappeared from the earth.

Fortunately, people had learned to work together and, because they had hands, had started using simple tools like tree branches for clubs and sticks for digging roots. They had learned to throw stones as weapons for hunting and for defence. Sometimes they used stones as hammers. Even more fortunately, people were curious and learned from experience. Better still, they had speech and so had a way of teaching each other, even if their language only had a few words.

In Sim's clan there were about twenty-seven members. About half of them were children. Father was called Dedu, which meant "good hunter." When he was a young man, he usually hunted alone. He would follow a group of hyenas, the best of the animal hunters, for days until they had killed an antelope or some medium-sized animal. When they had eaten, and temporarily left their kill, he would snatch away as much of the carcass as he could carry, and return to the home cave as quickly as possible. Sometimes he would be followed by a pack of hyenas. For safety he would have to climb a tree and stay there until his pursuers got tired and left. Life for people was very hard and very, very dangerous and very short in length.

It was because of Father's habit of following hyenas that he met Mother. One day, he spied two trying to capture something they had chased up a small tree. Since there were just two hyenas, Father thought that he could drive them away with his thick club and his throwing stones. He, then, could capture whatever they had treed. Getting as close as possible, he began hurling stones at them. One hyena, hit on the shoulder, ran away, yelping in pain. Making as much frightening noise as he could, Father ran toward the other with his club raised. It turned tail and fled.

Looking up to find out what had captured the interest of the hyenas, he discovered a frightened young woman, a stranger, looking down at him with terrified eyes. Father signalled her to come out of the tree. After hesitating a bit, she did, just as the two attackers returned. The young woman bent down, picked up one of Father's stones and hurled it at the lead hyena. To his amazement, she was very good at throwing. When her stone not only hit but knocked one hyena down, the other ran off. Father killed the injured animal with his club.

Together they skinned the carcass, or rather she did, using a sharp stone knife. Father had never seen a cutting tool before. He knew only throwing stones and stones that could be used as hammers. His people had to use their teeth for cutting and tearing to remove any animal skin. This new cutting tool the woman used made this tough job much much easier. Once finished, she took the hyena meat that could be carried by the two of them and wrapped it up in the fresh still-bloody skin. Hyena meat was not very good for eating, but it was food.

The woman put her flint knife into a little skin sack worn around her neck and wiped her hands on some grass to remove the blood. Together, they headed back to Father's home cave. By following a route that would keep them close to trees, they could spend the nights up high in the branches, safe from the meat eaters who hunt in the dark.

This stranger, separated from her people, lost and hungry, was thankful to have found a friendly man. At first they could only talk with hand gestures, but since both their

languages were very simple, she soon learned to speak
Father's tongue. When they arrived at his home cave, they
stayed together as mates.

Mother was very different from the women at the home
cave. More slender and taller than the other women, she
was as tall as the men, the fastest runner, the best climber,
and by far the best stone thrower. Most importantly, she
was very curious and quickly learned where good eating
roots could be found. She knew how to cure animal skins
and made Father a cloak from the hyena skin. He was now
the only person in his clan to have a predator skin to wear.
Other hunters would never dare to attack these dangerous
beasts. Also, Mother was the only woman who had her own
possessions. In the skin bag around her neck, she kept
special things, her carefully chosen smooth round stones for
throwing and her precious flint knife.

At first, the other women did not like Mother because
she was different and because she did things that they could
not. However, they soon discovered that she was willing to

help them with many things, particularly with taking care of injuries. In many ways she became popular, but since she was a stranger, they were never completely comfortable with her.

The thing that probably made her most admired was food. After a successful hunt, it was the custom for the men to eat first. They took the best parts of the raw meat and ate as much as they could. This meant that the women and children and the few older people had very little left for them. But because Mother was so good with the throwing stones, she frequently killed a rabbit or squirrel or a water bird close to home and always shared this meat with the hungry ones. She did this when the men were off on hunts. Gradually, the other women, in some ways, began to treat her the way they did the men.

After a while Mother became pregnant and, some time later, a girl was born. Two years afterwards, a boy was born. When he was old enough to begin walking, his left foot could not bend up at the ankle. He was never able to walk like others, but always moved with a hopping limp. That was when the people began to call him "Sim," and gave Mother another name, "Shim," which meant "mother of the lame one."

The grown-ups in the cave group acted as if Sim were not there. Babies with problems were always put out to die. They simply could not understand why Mother and Father had not done the same with the lame boy. This practice was not cruelty, but cave people knew that any creature that could not look after itself could not survive. The old and badly injured were treated the same way. That is how all animals treat the helpless; they do not necessarily kill them, they just do not help them. In a time of very little food, they drive away those that cannot fend for themselves.

Eevo, his big sister, protected Sim and kept him from being hit by the other children. In this case, she had help from two slightly older girls called Ree and Ur. Sim liked them all, especially his sister. They became very close and the best of friends.

Because Father was a superior hunter, Sim had more to eat than most, and he grew tall and strong in comparison to the others. Although some of the adults still felt Sim should have been put out of the clan, they left him alone, not wanting to have Dedu angry with them. Mother taught Sim how to throw and he too became very good. But what Sim did best was watch and learn.

But now with Father and Mother gone, some members of the clan, saying there would not be enough food for winter, had chased Sim away. Ab, Father's friend, and Ro the other injured hunter, had tried to stop them, but were ignored. Sim, frightened and alone, had tried to come back to the cave but again was driven away. After staying as close to home for as long as he could, he slowly limped away, tears running down his face. How would he survive? The morning was still early, the sun just rising in the sky as he reluctantly hobbled off into a land he did not know.

Sim was huddled in a small clump of trees a few hundred paces from the cave, when a sudden noise startled him. Jumping to his feet, he turned, expecting to see some fierce animal about to pounce on him. But fright changed to relief. The noise was Eevo, hurrying toward him. She had a bag like Mother's hanging around her neck. In her hand she carried a sack. It was Father's hyena skin and inside were some roots. Eevo had left the safety of the cave to join her brother. Together they would find somewhere to live, some way to survive.

Two

The Tree-Eating Animal

Eevo and Sim knew they were in very great danger. Feeling very much alone, they headed away from their home cave. Sim's face was streaked with tears and dirt. His shoulder hurt from being hit by a stone. He was still very scared, but grateful for Eevo's presence. But what were they to do?

"Where will we go?" he asked.

Eevo, too, was very frightened and, being older, knew that their chance of surviving even one night in the open, was poor. She tried to hide these thoughts from Sim.

"We must find a place to stay," she replied. "Father would say, 'Stay in the tree area, so that you can climb to safety' or he would say, 'Find a small cave and block the entrance with rocks.' He told us these things. Remember?"

This positive talk encouraged Sim. Remembering Father's advice meant that they now had a plan. All that day, the children walked, pausing only to drink from a stream.

The sun was beginning to set. Soon large hunting animals would come out for their usual evening search for food. Eevo and Sim had just reached the border of the tree country when they saw a small opening in the side of a wooded hill. Ahead stretched open grassland. They headed for the cave, remembering Father's advice.

The narrow entrance was so tiny they could barely squeeze through. Once inside, Eevo pulled a rock across the opening, making it much too small for any dangerous animal. They ate some of the roots that Eevo had brought, then, exhausted from the day's happenings, they snuggled together to keep warm, and went to sleep.

During the night a storm blew up with gale-force wind and pelting rain. The sharp bright bolts of lightening and loud claps of thunder terrified the brother and sister. They clung to each other and cowered in the cave. A sudden bright flash followed immediately by a great crash of thunder left them deaf for a moment. Then, as quickly as the storm had come, it passed. The rain stopped, but the rock at the mouth of the cave had a flickering light around it. The cave seemed to be getting warmer. The children were puzzled and cautiously peered out. What was this bright light? This heat?

Right outside, a tree struck by lightening was burning fiercely, flames crackling and leaping in the darkness of the night. Sim and Eevo drew back, still clinging together, as frightened as before. What was this strange new beast?

As they watched, the fire continued to burn but did not try to get into the cave. Gradually, it stopped being something to fear. Its warmth was even pleasant. Eevo rolled the rock away from the mouth of the cave and the two crawled out with care. Being curious children born of a curious mother and father, they watched what the fire was doing.

"It's eating the tree," Sim said.

Eevo said nothing, but studied it intently. Suddenly, the children realized that they were standing out in the open at night. They could see one another easily. This meant that the hunting animals could see them too. But nothing bad had happened, even though they had been standing outside for some time. This was very strange.

Finally Eevo spoke, "Remember how frightened we were at the first sight of this tree-eating animal? If we could have, we'd have run away. But we were trapped in the cave. The big hunters of the night must be frightened too. If we stay close to this hot-light animal, whatever it is, they will not come close. I know that if I saw a tree-eating animal that is hotter than the hottest sunlight in summer, I would stay away too."

"Do you suppose that it lives in the clouds and got hungry and jumped down to eat the tree?" asked Sim.

Eevo continued thinking out loud, "Could this be what Mother told us lived at her home cave? The thing that people fed regularly so it would stay healthy and not leave? It kept dangerous animals away. They called it Fire."

She pulled Sim's elbow. "Maybe we should move back a bit. I'm getting too warm, but I want to stay close to see what it does."

Sim pointed to a smaller fire that had started in a bunch of leaves and twigs close to them. "Look, it's having babies!"

This tiny fire was not so hot, so they moved nearer and watched even more carefully. By now they had become quite confident in believing that the fire did not want to eat them and that it was keeping the hunting animals away. If only they could get it to stay with them!

They squatted down and watched. The small fire flared up rapidly when it came to some dried grass and then, when the grass and twigs were burned, it began to die down.

"It is dying the way some of the little children in the cave do when there is not enough food," said Sim.

Eevo reached down and picked up a handful of leaves and grass and dropped it on the dying embers. Rapidly, the grass and leaves caught fire and flared up again, almost as if to say, "thank you" to the children. Once more, as that fuel was used up, the small fire began to die down. Eevo and Sim began to gather leaves and twigs, and then some larger sticks, and put these on the fire. And again, the fire came back to life.

"It eats the loose stuff quickly, but takes longer to eat the bigger pieces," reasoned Eevo.

"Let's gather some big sticks to feed it."

Just then there was a sharp crack. A small red ember popped out of the fire and landed near Sim's feet. He reached down to pick it up.

"Ow!" he hollered. "It bites!" He stuck his singed fingers into his mouth, "The big animals must know that, so they are afraid of it. That piece was only a little one, but its bite really hurts."

The fire was exciting, but Sim was very tired. When Eevo suggested he crawl back into the little cave, he did.

With his sore fingers in his mouth, he was soon fast asleep.

Some time later he awoke, looked about and leapt up in fright. The tree-eating animal was in the cave. He started to escape outside when he saw his sister coming towards the mouth of the cave, carrying a bundle of sticks. He shouted to warn her.

"It's in, it's in!"

Sim was almost angry when she calmly said, "I know. I brought it in while you were asleep. After you went inside, I watched the fire for a while. Now I know what it eats. It doesn't eat stones or earth, but it does like wood, dry grass and dry leaves. It will eat green leaves and grass but does not like them as much as dry ones. And green sticks are eaten but it takes longer. It does not like water. Water makes it crackle. But I did find that if I put a dry stick into it, the part that was in the animal now has a new animal starting to grow on it. I now know to to move fire from one place to another. That's how I brought it inside."

Eevo paused to put her bundle down, and continued, "I don't think fire is really alive, but in many ways it seems to be. It moves and grows, and dies if it has no food, but it does not go to where its food is. It only eats the food it touches. It can get big very quickly if there is enough food, but unlike other animals it gets small if the food is used up. It is different from anything else we have seen. I thought that if we could have it come to live with us, it would keep us warm and protect us from the hunting animals. It is easy to feed as there is plenty of dry wood about, but it must be fed regularly. If it were to die we probably could not find another."

Sim was so interested that he lost his anger. He looked at Eevo and said, "But we have to go out to get food, roots and berries, eggs too, if we can find bird's nests. And we have to find a stream so that we can drink. If we stay here it will keep us warm, but we will starve. What shall we do?"

They both sat and looked at the fire. At last Eevo got up and said, "I will go out and try to find some food. It is now daytime and the night hunters have gone back to their dens. Watch the fire and feed it. I will be back as soon as I can. Then you can go to get a drink of water." After checking her supply of throwing stones, she left.

Sim sat near the mouth of the cave and watched the light from the fire. He was fascinated. Taking one of the longer straight sticks, he stuck the smaller end into the fire. It began to burn. He scraped the burning end along a rock and noticed that the scraping and rubbing put the fire out, but made black marks on the boulder. He looked at the burned end and found that it now came to a point and was darker in colour. It was still warm but, when he touched it quickly, it did not bite him the way the ember had done during the night. He stuck the point into the ground to see if it would be good for digging. It was. Moreover, the point stayed sharp. It was much harder than the wood had been before burning. It also had a new smell.

Sim looked up and saw that the tree was still burning, but the flames were not jumping as high as before. Suddenly, beyond the tree, he saw Eevo racing toward him, chased by hyenas, the pack almost at her heels.

Hyenas are among the best hunters known. They hunt in packs and can kill animals much bigger than themselves. Sim was scared but, even more, he was angry at the hyenas for chasing his sister. He grabbed a branch lying on the ground and shoved the leafy part into the large fire still devouring the tree. The leaves and small twigs, dried by the

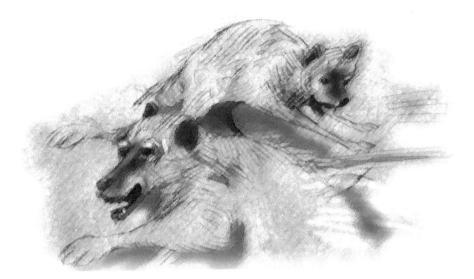

continuous heat of the burning tree, flared up quickly.
Waving the flaming branch before him, Sim headed for the
hyenas, running faster than he ever thought possible. He
shoved the flaming branch into the face of the first hyena,
then hit the second across the chest with his fiery weapon.

As hyenas have a coat of fairly long always greasy hair,
it ignited instantly. With their hairy coats in flame, the two
hyenas screamed in pain, turned and ran off, the others following. As they raced through dry grass and bushes, they
created a huge grass fire that quickly spread across the
grassland.

Eevo had left the cave to get water for herself and to
find food, any food. She had not gone far when she spotted
a rabbit running towards her. With a throwing stone from
her carrying bag, she killed it. As she picked up the rabbit,
she puzzled as to why it had been running out in the open.
The reason soon became very evident. Hyenas were chasing
it. Now it was Eevo who was in trouble. The hyenas, spot-
ting a new victim, headed in her direction. Since there was
no tree nearby for her to climb, she fled back the way she

had come, back toward the cave. Fast runner that she was, she increased the distance between the hyenas and herself.

"If I can get to the burning tree, with Sim's help I might have a chance," she thought. Almost exhausted, she saw Sim running toward her. "Why is he doing this? He knows that he is no match for more than one hyena." This added fear ran through her mind. Then she recognized what he was carrying.

"I hope it works," was all she could think when Sim charged at the first two animals. The defeat of the hyenas delighted her. As she caught her breath, she thought to herself, "If we can keep fire, we will not have to run and hide from these night hunters."

But, seeing the grass on fire and the huge blaze that followed, Sim and Eevo realized that fire was not always a good friend. If not watched carefully, it could do great harm. Fortunately, because the land in front of the cave had been burned over the night before, there was no grass left there to catch fire. The two of them were safe.

In all the excitement Eevo had dropped the dead rabbit. It had landed in the embers of the fire still burning the tree. They smelled something strange, a smell that made them hungry. Eevo looked down and, remembering her kill, exclaimed, "Oh, the fire has eaten the rabbit!" She was about to reach for what was left when Sim stopped her.

"It will bite you hard," he said. Using his pointed stick, he flipped the blackened rabbit out of the hot coals. His sister almost cried. "All that food gone! Well, the fire did save us. Maybe it deserves the rabbit."

Sim said, "The fire has made it smell good and bad at the same time. Let's see it there is any left, or did fire eat it all."

Carefully, he poked at the little burned body with the point of his stick and was surprised when the blackened and hardened skin cracked. Inside the skin was roasted rabbit. Never had they tasted meat that was so good and so easy to eat. After chewing up every last bit, cracking the bones and sucking out the marrow, they were thirsty. The whole outside world looked black and was hot underfoot, but they walked quickly to the stream Eevo had found. After a long drink, they promptly returned to the cave. Even their hard thick-skinned feet were beginning to feel unpleasantly hot.

The rest of the day was spent in front of their cave, feeding their fire. That night they took turns sleeping, tending to the fire as Mother had told them her people did. The next morning the children explored the entire valley, now empty of animals because of yesterday's burn.

Returning to the stream, they followed it to its beginning and discovered it was a large spring coming from a rock wall. There was a cave in this rock face, a small climb up from the lower ground. Inside was another spring. This second spring filled a fairly deep depression in the floor of the cave, creating a clear pool of clean running water near the entrance. The overflow from it continued as the small flow of water that ran from the cave mouth and joined the larger stream that Sim and Eevo had followed.

This cave was roomy and there was an opening to the outside, high up in the rock face. The cave mouth was high enough and wide enough to allow easy entry. Before now they would not have wanted such a large opening, but now with their fire they would be safe. This was a perfect cave for a home.

On the top of the rock wall was a wooded area where

they could easily get wood to feed their fire. On the rocky ledges above the cave they saw many birds. Nests would be nearby where they could find eggs and, perhaps, even capture the occasional bird to eat.

Realizing that they had been away from the precious fire for some time, they hurried back to the small cave. The tree was still smoking and still too hot to approach closely. The small fire at the mouth of the cave was a bed of red hot coals, but without flames.

"The fire's hungry," said Sim, and he put some small sticks on the embers. When they did not flare up at once, the way the dried grass had, Sim bent over the fire to see what was happening. Accidentally, he breathed in some smoke and began to cough. His coughing blew away some of the ashes and made the hot embers glow hotter and brighter. The fresh wood caught fire and flames began to dance.

"It likes to be blown on," he noted. Sim began blowing on the coals and the extra air made the fire burn brighter. Something new had been learned about this mysterious force.

The children decided to live in the new larger cave, but how were they to move the fire? Eevo had an plan. They would carry a supply of wood to their new home. Since the grass fire of the previous day had burned every stick of wood between the two caves, they would put plenty of wood on to their existing fire. They could come back to it if something went wrong.

Each would take a burning stick from the fire and walk toward the new cave for as long as the sticks burned well. Then, using the burning stubs of these sticks, they would build a fire with wood from the bundle they were carrying.

18

They would wait until this new fire was burning well, then take the best sticks out of this new fire, and continue walking toward the new cave. They would repeat this as often as needed.

Their plan worked. The burning sticks lasted longer than they thought possible. Only one fire needed to be made along the way. Once inside the new cave, they built their home fire with care. When the smoke rose, they noticed that the hole up near the roof of the cave made an excellent chimney, letting the smoke escape.

Once certain that their new fire was burning well, Eevo and Sim went up the hillside to gather more wood. While picking up fuel for the fire, they disturbed a number of birds, scaring them from their nests along the rocky ledges. Some of the nests contained eggs. Eevo and Sim ate them, right on the spot.

What a strange pair they made! Their faces, streaked with soot from the fire and dripping with egg yolk, were decorated with large yellowy-black egg mustaches. Their stomachs now full, Sim and Eevo returned to their new cave with armloads of wood and drank some water from the small spring gushing out of the rock wall. They lay down for a short sleep, both feeling warm, comfortable and safe. It had been a wonderful day.

In three days time, the two of them had changed. Instead of being frightened children, watching fearfully for any danger lurking about them, they had become confident. They were still cautious, but no longer afraid of every shadow. The grass fire, which had been a very large one, had driven away the grass eaters. Now, because there were no grass eaters nearby there were no meat eaters. This whole area belonged to the children, at least for the time being.

Eevo woke with a start. Something was touching her face. It was Sim's finger and he was drawing in the soot that had made her face black. He laughed when she got up, "You should see yourself. The black and yellow streaks make you look funny."

"You're pretty odd yourself," said Eevo. Remembering the pool at the cave mouth, she went to it and looked down into the water. There she saw her reflection and giggled. She splashed some water on her face. Sim had been watching all this with interest. Suddenly, a big grin appeared on his face. Quietly, he came up behind his sister, put his hands on her bottom and pushed her into the pool.

She squealed and splashed and, scrambling out of the pool, chased him around the cave. Catching Sim's arm, Eevo pushed him in, then jumped in herself. It was great fun; the first time they had ever been in water, although Sim did not stay long. Eevo took some sand and rubbed it over the very dirty spots on her body and hair, then rinsed off. She climbed out, shook her head to get some water out of her hair, and went to the fire to warm up and dry. Sim watched, quietly.

He came up to his sister and squatted beside her. He touched her skin which now felt different. She was clean for the first time in her life. "Do you know," he said, "you don't smell much anymore? If I came up to you in the dark I would not know that you were there."

"It feels good too," said Eevo. "Why don't you do the same." And he did. Feeling sleepy again, he sat down near the fire and watched the flames flickering on the rock wall of the cave. Life felt very good.

Three

Flint Works

The days were still quite warm, but the nights were beginning to be colder. Even though the sun was lower on the horizon, the children had not noticed the change. While the burned-over grassland was becoming greener, the grass was still very short. Only a few grazing animals had returned to feed, but none of the large meat eaters. As the shrubs recovered from the big blaze, mice and rabbits moved back. This food supply, of course, brought in the smaller predators: the hyenas, wolves, foxes and weasels.

To this list were added two new predators, Sim and Eevo. From the time they had watched the burning hyenas fleeing from them, they had begun to lose their terrible fear of all the smaller predators. Now they, too, were hunters, able to live very well on rabbit that their well-thrown stones had killed. This food, along with eggs collected from the nests on the cliffside, plus root vegetables and berries, made a very good diet.

Both young people began to grow taller and stronger, growth that should have come earlier, but had not because of poor food at the home cave.

From time to time, especially while skinning a rabbit with her teeth, Eevo missed the use of a knife. How very useful it had been! One day Sim decided to do something to help. He had seen his father's knife many, many times and knew the type of flat grey stone used to make one. The sides looked as if chips of stone had been broken off, leaving each edge with a ragged appearance but very sharp to the touch. With repeated use, these sharp edges had broken off and gradually the knife had become dull, until it was no longer any good for cutting.

It was for this reason that Father and Mother had gone, to find people who knew the secret of flint chipping. Mother's father was a master flint knapper, but they didn't know if he was still alive. It was likely she would have a good chance of getting a new knife from her people, but Father, if he went alone, especially as a stranger, would probably have less chance. Making a good flint knife required much skill and time.

From the base of the cliff Sim gathered a number of flint stones that looked suitable. They were embedded in soft white stone that broke away easily from the harder flint. Next he found some different rocks to use as a hammer for breaking up these pieces. What he did not know was that flint was much harder than his hammer stones. All that happened when he worked, was that Sim ended up with banged-up fingers. Whenever he hit the flint with his awkward hammer, it was this rock that would break. The flint remained whole.

After a day spent in bruising his hands, Sim became quite frustrated. Picking up the flint piece he had been pounding, he hurled it as hard as he could against a large black rock at the mouth of the cave. To his surprise, the flint shattered into many pieces, a number of them with very sharp edges. Some could be used for cutting skins. Some could also be used to cut the tough marsh rushes needed to pad the rock floor, making a more comfortable bed for both of them.

Sim was delighted with his good luck. Among the broken pieces of flint were three larger pieces with long sharp edges that, although not as neat as father's knife, could be very useful. Eevo made a neck pouch like hers for Sim to wear. Now each had a knife to carry. The third piece was kept near the fire to make wood shavings for rekindling the embers quickly whenever the flames became very low.

The fire was never in danger of going out, but sometimes they would use softer wood that burned more rapidly. Although there were always plenty of hot coals left, they were not pleased until they saw flames merrily dancing on the wood. It was then they knew that their friend, the fire, was happy.

In many ways the brother and sister had continued to change, although they were not aware of it. The other animals around them, however, did notice, but, of course, they could not talk, and so did not tell them in words. But they did tell them through their animal behaviour. When Sim and Eevo had been driven away from the home cave, they were terrified. They walked in a fearful way, moving from tree to tree, always seeking shelter. Because they were afraid, their fear created a certain smell telling other predators that these were animals to be hunted. However, after the defeat of one of their most feared enemies, the hyenas, all this watching for danger changed. Now, with their freedom from fear, they walked in the confident manner of the hunter. No longer were they the hunted. They remained cautious, but it was the caution of the hunter taking care that the animal being stalked did not see him. Their goal was to become better hunters. The other predators recognized this and kept their distance, especially the hyenas who remembered what the children could do.

Sim, sitting by the fire during one of his periods of fire watching, and playing as usual with burning sticks, remembered something. It was the digging stick he had made by hardening its tip in the fire that first day.

'Why,' he thought, 'don't I get a long straight stick and harden the tip in the fire. Then, if I can get close to a small grass eating animal, I could use the stick like a long tooth. We would have more food and better skins to help us keep warm.'

Putting more wood on the fire, he woke his sister and told her what he wanted to do. Ever since Sim had succeeded in making the flint knives, Eevo had stopped saying, "Don't be silly, Sim" when he came up with a new idea. She had begun to listen carefully to him.

It was just beginning to be light outside. "Let us go and gather some eggs and some wood and we can look for some good long sticks," she said. "If they don't work out, they can always be fed to the fire."

Dawn was a good time to collect eggs as the birds left their nests early to look for food. But, as the cold season was approaching, there were fewer and fewer eggs. During their search for more food, Sim found a few four or five-year-old trees. After much hacking with his knife and pulling with all his strength, he was able to loosen them.

Triumphantly, he dragged the saplings back home.

Once inside the cave, he trimmed off the branches, removed the bark and put the thinner ends into the fire. He made sure that the part he burned was about as thick as his wrist. This fresh wood, however, was green and was slow to catch fire. When finally a stem was almost burned through, he removed it from the fire and began to scrape off the singed part. Once finished, Sim had five sticks with hard sharp points, each a little less than twice his height.

Eagerly, they tried these sharpened poles for digging and, although they were a little long, each one worked. From that time on, Eevo and Sim always took their sharp sticks with them whenever hunting. By pretending that they were using them for sticking at animals, they practised handling these long digging sticks as though they were spears. But for the next little while not even one small grass eater came into view.

Four

Wolves

About a month before Eevo and Sim found their new home, an older pregnant wolf had made a home for herself on the slope of a hillside, on the same escarpment as their cave. It was rather late in the year for her to be giving birth. The male wolf, her mate, had been killed in a fight with one of the large cats whose hunting area the wolves had invaded. Alone, she had given birth to three cubs, two females and a male.

Without a mate, she was having a most difficult time looking after her cubs and hunting for food, for them and herself. The cubs were still nursing, but beginning to eat the meat she would regurgitate for them. Food for three cubs meant that she got very little for herself. Then came the fire that the hyenas had spread, but for which Sim was really responsible. As a result, there were no grass eaters to be found. Even mice were scarce.

She was not the only one short of food. The hyenas, the survivors of the encounter with Sim, were desperately hungry. And so it happened. One day, while the wolf was out hunting, two hyenas found and entered her den. The three little cubs, huddling in the very back part, whimpered in fear. Although the little male tried to fight back, he was killed almost instantly. With the limp cub clutched in its jaws, one hyena left the den, knowing that the mother wolf was close by. Better get away before she returned.

Its starving mate, rather than grab one of the remaining babies, tried to snatch the dead cub. A fierce fight began. The mother wolf, alerted by the noise, raced back to her den and clamped her jaws on the throat of the hyena holding her dead cub. The second hyena snuck up behind her and grabbed her back leg, tearing the hamstring muscles. The crippled wolf fought on.

Eevo and Sim, out on an egg and bird hunting trip, heard the growls and snarls of the nearby deadly struggle. A few weeks earlier they would have hidden, but now with their new-found confidence, they headed towards the commotion. Sim, when he saw the female wolf fighting the two hyenas and the tiny dead wolf cub on the ground, felt a rage similar to his feelings when the hyenas were chasing Eevo. Without hesitation, he threw a stone at the hyena tearing the wolf's leg, striking it in the shoulder. Immediately he rushed toward it. The sudden sharp pain from the stone made the hyena release its hold on the wolf, but only to face its new attacker, Sim.

The hyena felt trapped. As the only way out was to get past Sim, it leapt at him. Sim tensed, braced the thick end of the spear on the ground and dropped the point to meet the hyena's charge. The spear pierced its chest wall and tore through its heart, killing it instantly. Pulling his stick free,

Sim stepped back. He was shaking, more with excitement than fear. His sharp stick had made him much stronger than one of the better hunters! He had killed the hyena!

Eevo hurried forward with her stick, but, seeing that her help was not needed, she hugged Sim with relief.

Meanwhile, the wolf, now that the enemy from behind was dead, picked up the hyena she had grabbed. With a quick shake, she broke its neck, killing it. Sim and Eevo turned their attention to the mother wolf. Although badly hurt, she was still a dangerous animal. But the wolf had no thought of attacking them. With pain-filled eyes she looked back at them and, picking up her dead cub, slowly dragged herself into her den.

The next day, and the day after, Eevo and Sim returned to check on the mother wolf. On the third day, they found her dead, with the two remaining little cubs still trying to

nurse. Had the children followed the custom of people at that time, they would have killed the two cubs for food. But they could not do that.

"She and I fought the hyenas together," said Sim. "Now, what shall we do with her babies? We have no milk for them."

"We have eggs," replied Eevo. Scooping up a cub in each hand, she held them warmly against her chest. Sim carried their sticks, the wonderful weapons he had made, and followed his sister back to their home. Eevo fed the cubs with eggs, which they liked, then gave them bits of the same food that she and Sim had been eating. The cubs, their bellies full, lay down in front of the fire as if it were something they had always done and fell fast asleep.

Sim sat and looked at his sharp sticks, which they now called spears. He felt the points and scraped them a bit more to make them even sharper. He did not notice that his sister was gone until she returned carrying the two hyena skins and also the wolf skin.

"I didn't know what to do about the wolf," she said. "But I think the cubs, if they smell their mother on you and me, will feel more at home. So even if I didn't like to, I skinned her and brought her fur back. Anyway, these skins are far warmer than the rabbit skins we have, and will help us keep warm."

For the next few days the cubs followed whichever of the two wore the wolf skin. Then, as the smells of all living things in the cave blended, they began to consider themselves members of the cave pack.

The cubs grew very rapidly and ate a lot, so much so that one day Sim was heard to say, "Now I understand why

the clan chased me away. It's hard getting enough food for
those two little ones." But, in another two months, the
instincts of the wolves made themselves known. The two
cubs, although still spending most of their time playing and
wrestling with each other and with the children, began to
hunt. At first it was mice and later on other small animals
like moles. Occasionally, they would try for a rabbit.

Now, with the wolf cubs in the cave, there was even
more change in the way Eevo and Sim lived. They had
taken on the responsibility of looking after two young animals whose instincts were completely different from those
of people. These were wild animals which, even if they had
no contact with other wolves, were still wolves. Wolves are
animals genetically programmed to be wolves. Instinctively,
they are used to the social structure of the wolf pack. This
means obeying the lead or Alpha wolf of the pack. They

were born with instincts that can not change.

The children, too, were programmed by their species. They were family animals. Because humans have such a long growing-up period, the older children are programmed to be responsible for the young in the group and to cooperate with the group. Hence, they tried to treat the wolves as they would the young children in the clan and the wolves treated Sim and Eevo as they would the dominant pack leaders. Somehow it worked out. Since the language the humans used had a small vocabulary, much communication was by hand signals and gestures. This the wolves could understand. Somehow the group became one family or clan or pack. The wolves understood the children and the children understood the wolves.

Such wonderful communication between human and wolf made hunting easy. The wolves would drive the hunted animal toward the humans and, if the spears failed, as often happened, the wolves would bring the animal down. Such a partnership meant more food for everybody. With the harsh winter weather coming, the thought of hunting being much more difficult had worried Sim and Eevo. Now, with the help of the wolves, hunting was as good as in the warm periods.

The fire, always well-fed with wood, kept them much warmer than they would have been without it. Usually, winter meant starvation and misery from the cold. But now, however, the hunting skills Sim and Eevo had developed, plus the skills the wolves brought, meant plentiful food for all four and warm clothing for Eevo and Sim.

Throughout the winter the cubs grew rapidly and, at six months of age, were heavier and bigger than the children. Wolves, at two years of age, can weigh about 150 pounds and these cubs were now more than half grown. Despite their size difference, the wolves continued to accept the children's leadership, the leadership of their Alpha animals.

Both Sim and Eevo were growing too. While living in the home cave, they had experienced constant hunger. Even though their father was a good hunter, there was never enough food. Now, with plenty to eat at all times, they had become taller and stronger than most adults of their clan. Sim, who now was about 11 years of age, was as tall as the average man of his home clan. Eevo had also grown. They, of course, did not know this. They could only measure themselves against each other and since both were growing at about the same rate, they were not aware of the change.

Sim had such great hope that his spears would make it possible to hunt almost anything. He had even tried them on fish in the larger stream. Once he learned to aim below, rather than right at a fish, Sim had more success. For some reason that he could not understand, the spear looked as if it bent up when he thrust it into the water. In warm weather, however, Eevo's method of catching was better. She would just stand in the stream with her hand underwater and her fingers moving slowly. Before long, a fish would approach. Eevo would let it examine her hand, keeping up the slow finger movements, gently tickle its belly and then, with a quick scoop of her hand, flip the fish out on to the shore.

Sim continued to want to improve his spears. Often he was disappointed because they were just not good enough. Once his spear bounced off an antelope which, in turn, knocked him down. While not hurt, he was embarrassed. Something had to be done.

One day, coming back from the fishing area, by chance he noticed a tree that had been pulled down during a landslide after a heavy rain. It had been pounded by the falling rocks and the trunk had split apart, exposing the core. From this part of the tree, Sim was able to get some long straight pieces of wood. He dragged them back to the cave for future use.

For some time now, the days were becoming longer and the cold period was expected to end soon. Usually their area had little snow, but this year was different. One grey morning it began to snow heavily, but since they had plenty of meat and plenty of firewood, they remained in the cave while the blizzard howled outside. Eevo softened skins and laboriously sewed them into cloaks and pants. The wolves slept. Sim worked on making a new spear from the wood of the split tree. By chipping and scraping, he made a shaft just a little longer than Eevo's height. He had found that his earlier spears were much too long and too heavy. He smoothed the wood to make his spear as straight as he could.

But how to make a spear sharper? Sim had an idea. He scraped a deep notch into one end of the spear. Then, look-ing through his collection of flint chips, he found one he liked. Using a hard throwing stone as a hammer, he chipped off a bit until it fit into the notch. He picked up some gut saved from the last antelope they had killed (the one that had embarrassed him but was brought down by the wolves). The string of gut was used to tie the flint tightly into the notch at the end of the spear. This was something new. Would this new weapon work? Sim was anxious to find out, but the storm kept them penned inside.

This new spear, made from wood that was dry, was lighter than the previous ones made from saplings. It felt good in his hand. Eevo liked it too. With the miserable weather continuing and, with no need to hunt, they decided

34

to make more spears like the new one. Eevo was working on a spear shaft and had trimmed it to about the size she wanted. The wood, however, was rough with many sharp splinters. Taking one of the softer kind of stones, the kind that breaks when you hit it against a hard stone like flint, she began to rub it rapidly along the shaft. When she felt it for smoothness, she found, to her surprise, that the surface was warm.

'How did that happen?' she thought. 'It has not been near the fire.' She continued to rub the shaft and checked it again. Once more it was quite warm. When she told Sim about this, they wondered if fire lived inside the wood. Perhaps that was why fire became bigger when they put fresh wood on it. Then, busy trying to finish the spears, they forgot about this mysterious heat.

Next day the snow stopped falling and they awoke to a silent world. Everything was draped in white, a beautiful snowscape glittering in the sunlight. All four went out and played, leaping into high drifts, sliding down slopes. The wolves pushed their noses into the huge piles of snow, then, throwing back their heads, tossed a spray of white flakes over their bodies.

Eevo went back into the cave and put a big pile of wood on the fire. She picked up a skin bag of dried meat and a torn skin used for dragging wood back home. Slinging them both over her shoulder, she picked up four of the new and as yet untried spears and went outside. Calling the others, she suggested a hunt for fresh meat and a wood gathering, their first outing for some days.

Rather than take their usual route over the grassland, they headed into the wooded area. This way would take them through lots of trees, a space without the huge windswept drifts that covered the flat grassland area. And thus it was that, unintentionally, they found themselves heading towards their former home.

Ghosts

It was a perfect day for a hunt, sunny and bright with animal tracks easy to see in the glistening snow. Finally, Sim had a chance to use his new flint-tipped spear. When the wolves scared a large hare out of the bushes, he speared it with ease. He was delighted!

With great hunting success and excellent weather encouraging them, Eevo and Sim continued their trek through the trees. All of a sudden, the wolves stopped frolicking. The hair on their backs rose in a warning ridge and a soft rumbling growl came from deep in their throats. Eevo and Sim became alert. All four moved forward with care. Just over a rise of land, they could see something struggling through the snow. It was a strange man carrying a thick stick club, the kind Father used to take when he went hunting. But this man was on his own. Something was wrong!

unters, with the exception of Father, never hunted
. In some ways the human began to look familiar as
y moved closer, but it was not Father. The wolves,
meanwhile, had begun their circular movement that would
place them behind the man, one wolf on each side, their
usual manoeuvre for driving animals towards Eevo and
Sim.

Eevo was first to recognize the stranger. He was Ab,
Father's close friend, one of the two clan's hunters, injured
by hyenas just before Sim was driven away. She called to
the wolves to stop, but they were too intent on stalking their
prey to hear her.

With Sim behind her, Eevo raced towards the man, hoping to prevent the wolves from attacking. Aware of sounds
of movement around him, Ab looked up to see two large
strangers running toward him. As he turned to escape, he
saw two wolves bounding at him from the other direction.
Death seemed inevitable, but he was determined to put up a
battle. Suddenly, he heard one of the well-bundled strangers
calling out to him. "Ab, stop! Stop!"

Ab lowered his club and stared. Knowing that the
wolves were closing in, he turned and ran in the direction
of the stranger who called his name. Eevo, the speedier of
the two, reached him before Sim. The two wolves, almost
upon their prey, stopped abruptly when Eevo's hand signal
told them that this was not an animal to hunt. But they
stayed on guard, ready to attack.

Somehow Ab was different, thought Eevo. He had been
much bigger when she had left the home cave. This Ab was
shorter, only about as tall as Sim.

Ab was confused, and very hungry, and very tired.
Trapped by the storm of two or three days ago, or maybe

even more, he was no longer sure of himself. Now these unknown images were mocking him. Imagine a woman dressed for the cold with many fine skins! And, completely impossible, a woman who had her hand on the neck of a wolf larger than herself, with another huge wolf standing beside her.

Next, a large man, equally well-dressed, was approaching. He was a very successful hunter, as shown by his clothes, but one who walked with a limp. This whole experience must be a dream brought on by his hunger and lack of sleep, and by the cold. Or else he was in the land of the dead and these were Eevo and Sim who had left the cave in the time before the falling leaves. Most surely they had been killed by predators that roamed the grasslands. Their spirits were here now that he was dead. Exhaustion took over and Ab fainted, his body crumpling in the snow. The wolves growled, but Eevo moved to his side just as Sim arrived.

"It's Ab," said Eevo, "but he seems so small. He was as big as Father, but now he's no taller than you. But he is heavier," she continued, struggling to move him.

"He seems to be asleep. Let's wake him," said Sim. "We can't leave him lying in the snow. With only one skin on, he must be very cold."

Despite their attempts, Ab only groaned. Now the children were faced with a problem. They could go to the home cave to try to get help, but it was some distance away. If they did that, their fire at home would likely go out before they could get back. Besides, the people at the home cave might not let them return. On the other hand, their own cave was less time away if they were travelling as usual, but now they had Ab to carry. Strong as they were, it would still be difficult.

While pondering this dilemma, Eevo remembered the hide that they had brought for dragging back heavy pieces of wood. After spreading it out on the snow, they rolled Ab on top and headed for home, pulling their load. The snow that had made walking difficult, made sliding the skin with Ab on it much easier, except when the wolves tried to join in the pulling. Even with a stop to gather a little wood, they were back at their cave well before nightfall.

The fire was still burning, a deep bed of glowing hot coals. They lay Ab down on their rush bed and covered him with furs. The warmth and the smell of food being roasted on the fire, along with Sim shaking him every so often, finally roused him. Ab opened his eyes and looked about.

The people he saw were Eevo and Sim. But they were far bigger than they should have been. They were reddish in colour and the cave he was in was not dark. Why? He could not understand. The wolves were wolves, but did not act in a threatening way. As if to prove that these were all spirits, he suddenly realized why it was not dark. He was lying beside a small part of the sun, being warmed by it. He must be dead and in the land of the dead.

But this was far more comfortable than the land of the living had been for him, especially in those last days during that terrible snow. Never had he experienced anything like this before! His hunting companions, who had been separated from him, were not here. They must still be living. The Spirit Eevo, who had been holding a strip of meat on a stick over the small sun, saw that he was awake and offered him the hot food. His mouth watered from the very smell of it. Biting into the cooked hare, he found it hot, soft and more delicious than any meat he had ever eaten while alive.

Being dead was very pleasant. His thoughts were interrupted by a question from Sim.

"Ab, have Mother and Father come back? We thought that they would come to look for us. When I first saw you, I thought that you were Father. But, thank goodness we found you. You were the only one in the home cave who wanted me to stay. All the others said that I was a useless mouth to feed."

Ab remembered, only too well. "Forcing you out was bad, but I could do nothing. I was hurt and useless as a hunter. I thought that Ro and I would be driven off too if things got worse. You ask about your parents. They have not come back. But if they had, how could they look for you? Both Eevo and you are dead and have been eaten by the meat eaters."

Eevo laughed. "We are not dead. Here we are in our cave sitting around our fire and giving you food. Do you think that dead people could do that?"

"But you must be," said Ab. "You left the cave more than seven moons ago. You were children. How could you survive and in that short time become as big as large adults?"

"I will tell you how," and Eevo proceeded to talk. Ab sat and stared in disbelief while tearing chunks of roasted meat with his teeth. After the story had been told and retold, and the food, the cave and especially the wolves proved that it was true, he told them how things were at the home cave. Everything was bad.

"The people were worried about not having enough food for the winter. They were right. Things got worse than anyone expected. All the babies born this year have died, the new mothers had no milk. By the time of the great snow-storm there was only enough dried root to last a few days. Ro, Og, Yo and I went out to try to get anything we could, anything at all. The ground was too hard to dig for roots and there were no small animals. We could see the huge deer, but they are too big for us to hunt. Then came the snow and I lost the others."

After listening to Ab's report of the horrible situation and the starvation their people were facing, Eevo replied in a gentle and generous manner, "Sleep now, Ab. Tomorrow, take our store of dried meat and fish and root vegetables back to the home cave. Sim and the wolves will go with you, but will leave you near the cave. I don't know how the wolves would react to a lot of people, but I do know that our people would be very frightened. I cannot go. It would take too long and our fire might go out. Let them know that we are alive and well. We will leave some more meat near the home cave after our next hunt."

"And take some of our furs to keep you warm, also one of my spears," added Sim.

A very tired and still perplexed Ab lay down by the fire. Quickly he fell into a deep sleep, probably the first sleep he ever had during his adult life where he did not have to stay partly alert because of ever-present dangers.

"Well," Sim said, "We are probably the best Ghosts he could have found. But should we send all our food? Sometimes we have come back from a hunt with nothing."

"Not since the wolves have been hunting with us," reminded Eevo.

After putting more wood on the fire, Sim went to sleep. Eevo would sleep after the next feeding of the fire. When the morning dawned bright and clear, the three people in the cave woke. Arising first, Sim stirred the fire, then added more wood. After stepping out of the cave and peeing, he came back to the pond, knelt down and washed.

Ab was astonished. None of the people he knew had ever deliberately got themselves wet and rubbed the water over their faces. However, having seen how successful the brother and sister were, he was willing to imitate them. Eevo was selecting a spear and rubbing a rough spot on it before giving it to Ab, another surprise for him. In this cave there did not seem to be woman's work and man's work. The two did any task that needed doing. In fact, Eevo seemed to make the major decisions. She, too, relieved her-self outside, then went to wash while Sim put strips of the hare meat on thin sticks and hung them over the fire.

The wolves stirred a little but continued to sleep. Ab examined the spear. It was not a club but a long sturdy shaft with a sharp flint point. So sharp that, when he touched it to see what it felt like, he nicked his finger and was surprised to see blood. Everything in that cave seemed so astonishing that soon he was not surprised by anything. He now knew that the pair were not ghosts. But how could they have grown so much in so short a time? When Eevo and Sim told him how the fire at the mouth of the cave kept out all predators, he wondered if the home cave could possibly have a fire too? But he was reluctant to ask. Besides, would the people know how to look after one?

Eevo startled him by answering the question he had been afraid to ask. She explained that if the fire pot they had made for carrying the fire worked well enough, she would try to carry fire to the home cave and teach the people how to care for it. But, she admitted, the wolves might be a problem. Anyhow, she did not think it wise to try this move until the warmer weather came. When snow did not cover the ground, firewood could be found more easily.

After preparing a large bundle of food from their supply in the cave, she told Ab and Sim to go, but reminded her brother to stay well away from the home cave with the wolves. As they left, she turned to the woodpile. There was something she wanted to do and she wanted to do it when alone.

Sim, Ab and the wolves travelled as rapidly as possible toward the home cave of the clan. Sim remembered it as a long walk and thought that it would seem even longer through the snow. He, however, had forgotten that the first walk had been made by a frightened little boy. Now, after his tremendous growth because of a good food supply at just the right age, he was much stronger. And, because the fear that had been present earlier was gone, he could move much faster.

As the sun got higher in the sky, Ab said that they were only a short distance from the cave area. Sim was thinking that he would return, leaving Ab to finish the journey, when much to his dismay, the wolves suddenly took off on a side trip of their own. They seemed to disappear.

It wasn't long before Sim knew exactly what was happening. Sounds of a large animal crashing through the bush could be heard, coming in their direction. Ab also paused. A very experienced hunter, but one who always had to be concerned about being hunted himself, he was attuned to danger. He looked about for a tree that might provide shelter for them both. Sim, with confidence in his own ability, and with his experience of having the wolves as hunting partners, no longer felt the need to look for ways to escape. "Ab," Sim explained, "the wolves are driving an animal towards us."

Sim, spear ready, faced the direction of the sound. Ab, however, was not so calm. His instincts shouted, "Find a tree and climb out of harm's way!" Here he was with a boy, only about eleven years old, who was getting ready to meet whatever was making the noise. His pride, however, overcame his urge to flee and he stayed beside Sim. The crashing sound came closer and closer. Suddenly, a large buck elk came bounding out of the thicket. It saw the two men, but in its experience, the two-legged creatures, were only annoyances, not dangerous.

The danger was behind, the pursuing wolves. The best route of escape was past the two-legged things, so the elk kept its course. Sim had been in this position before, but never with so large an animal and never using a flint-tipped spear. He stuck the shaft of his spare weapon into the snow and crouched down a little. Holding his spear firmly with both hands, he aimed for a spot just behind the elk's shoulder. He thrust forward. The sharp flint point penetrated the elk's chest and the animal faltered, its front legs buckling as it crumpled forward into the snow. Sim grabbed his second spear and, using the entire weight of his body, plunged the flint-tipped shaft into the doomed beast.

Ab, although amazed at what had just happened, still reacted as a hunter. He, too, also speared the animal. The sharpness of his new weapon astonished him. The fact that he had faced an animal five times bigger than himself suddenly struck him. That an eleven year-old boy had done so first was unbelievable! Even more impressive was the fact that two wolves regarded the boy as pack leader, and had chased the elk to him.

"The wolves will want to eat," said Sim, "and then they

will return to our cave with me. You go on to the home cave and bring as many of the clan as you can to carry the meat back. There is enough here for the rest of the cold time."

He added, "Because you slept in our cave, and now carry some of the wolves' smell and our smell, the wolves have accepted you. But they would not accept strangers. Make sure we are gone before you come back for the meat. I don't want the wolves upset, especially since Eevo is not here to help control them. When travelling is easier, Eevo and I will come to the cave with the wolves, and bring the fire in the fire pot. With all of us as visitors, the wolves may be easier to manage."

Ab thanked Sim and headed toward the home cave, shaking his head and muttering to himself about all the events he did not yet understand.

Sim slit open the animal's belly and removed the entrails. While the wolves were eating their fill, he started the process of skinning the animal. He made a number of cuts in the skin, to make it easier for Ab and the others to finish. Taking some of the fresh hide, he wrapped up a portion of the liver and a large chunk of meat to carry home. Together, the satisfied wolves and triumphant Sim made their way back to Eevo.

Ab, who had gone only a short distance, stopped to watch. When he saw Sim and the wolves leaving, he hurried on. Upon arrival at his home cave, he found the people much weaker and hardly able to move, with just barely enough strength to greet him. The other hunters had returned, but with only a scavenged bone and very little meat. His people were starving. Ab thought of the herds of deer to be found in the forest all around, but the people could not hunt them. Their hunting tools were useless against such large animals. And he thought of how Sim, although only a child, had shown him how easily one of them could be killed. There was enough meat in this one hunt to keep the whole clan well-fed for a month.

Ab called to Ro and Og. "Come, I have food enough for the rest of the cold season. I need help to bring it back. Sim and I have killed an elk. We must hurry and get the meat home before other animals get it."

Ro wearily lifted his head. "Ab, stop making that sort of joke. All of us are starving and you think that telling stories about a dead boy is funny. Everyone knows that Sim and Eevo died in the falling-leaf season."

"They did not! They are alive and well and have sent us food. See what I bring." Ab opened the pack. The sight of the food brought the people scrambling to his side.

Ab tapped Ro on the shoulder and said, "Ro, you and Og, come with me. We have fresh meat only a short walk from here."

"You," he called to one of the older boys, "get some of the older children and come along." The two hunters and several of the boys struggled up and followed him. In a few minutes they were at the site of the kill.

Already a hyena was nearby, but the smell of the wolves had made it keep its distance from the carcass. But now that people were approaching, the hyena tried to chase them away. People usually ran from hyenas. But not this time. One of them, brandishing a stick, ran toward it. This was not how things should be. The hyena, however, being a smart animal, left to search for other prey.

Ro and Og were also amazed. They would have thrown

stones and waved their clubs, but never would they have wanted to attack a hyena alone, and with only a light stick. They said so.

"This stick helped kill that elk," Ab pointed out.

"This elk was killed by a wolf pack," said Og. "You can see their tracks and can smell their scent."

Ab reminded him. "Those were Sim and Eevo's wolves."

The others thought Ab's mind had left him, but he had brought more food than anyone had ever seen at one time. He had led them to this newly-killed elk, a huge animal. The site of the kill showed signs of wolf, but it also had been partly skinned and there were cuts in the hide to make skinning easier. Something must have done it.

Ab said that it was Sim's work. He explained how the wolves had helped the children. As experienced hunters, they knew that Eevo and Sim could not have survived on their own. But they also knew that wolves might hunt people. But help them? Never! So whatever had killed the elk had to be some magical thing, perhaps the spirits of the dead children. But why would their spirits help the clan? Here was food enough for the rest of the cold time, but how could they carry it?

Again Ab surprised them. Reaching into a pouch, he took out a flint knife. He continued skinning the animal and cutting off portions of meat that could be carried by the weakened boys. Then, tying the rest of the elk to a cut sapling, he had Ro and Og lift it on to their shoulders, one in front and one behind, so the suspended remains could be carried back to the home cave. It was a load that taxed their remaining strength and they stumbled under the weight of their burden. Fortunately, the distance back to the cave was short.

The flint knife was real. Ab never had a knife. That convinced Og that Ab was most likely a ghost or spirit and that Ab had died on the hunt and that his ghost was helping the clan. He began to treat Ab in a very careful way. Ab, having had the same feeling when he first woke up in the children's cave, understood and began to laugh. If being a Ghost meant not having Og or Ro complain about all the heavy carrying they were doing while Ab was walking along carrying only his spear, then Ab was quite happy to leave things that way.

He thought to himself, "What will they say when they see how much the children have grown? What about when they see the wolves? When Eevo brings them the bit of the sun that she said she would, what will they do?"

At first the thought amused him. Then he realized that this was a very serious matter. Were the people ready for so much change? True, they would be happy with the food, but could they accept the rest? He remembered how they behaved when Sim's father had first brought the strange tall young woman to the cave. They could not accept her different ways. The thought that here was a woman who hunted was not acceptable. They never refused the food Shim gave them, but the other women resented her. Not only was she a stranger, but she had taken the best hunter, the best man of the clan as her mate.

Then there had been the problem of Sim. He was a damaged child and would be useless as a hunter, but Shim refused to put him out to die. The problem was settled only when Dedu, his father, the clan's top hunter, threatened to leave with his family. After that, they stopped complaining about Sim, but continued to mutter among themselves. They whispered that the reason the boy was lame was because his mother did not act the way a woman should. Ab, however, had always liked Shim and thought fondly of Dedu as someone who taught him to hunt.

When it became necessary for Dedu and Shim to leave to get a new knife, the people, as soon as it was certain that they had really gone, had driven Sim away. Eevo had gone too. If the people had waited until a time when food was scarce he, Ab, would have understood. But they had done this so soon after Dedu and Shim left. The leaves had hardly begun to change colour and there still were plenty of berries. Now it was Sim and Eevo who had saved the clan from starvation. It was funny in a way that the boy, who would never be able to hunt and provide food for himself, had on one hunt provided the clan with more food than they had ever had at one time. Not only was Sim a survivor and a good hunter, he was also one of those very special people, a maker of tools.

And, there was more. Eevo was going to give the clan that most wonderful of all things, the thing all the predators feared, a little bit of the sun to keep in their cave. The people would be warm and safe from animal attacks while they slept. For certain they would think that Sim and Eevo were spirits, as they even now suspected Ab to be. That, however, had its advantages and Ab was not going to do anything to change those thoughts.

Six

Two Pieces of Wood

For Eevo and Sim, leaving the cave for any length of time had always been a problem. The fire needed frequent attention from them. To date they had only solved this predicament once. The moving of the fire from the original burning tree to their new home by carrying burning sticks and a bundle of firewood had worked well. But this would not work for travelling any big distance.

Some time before, Sim had made a basket from coarse rushes like the ones used for their bed, and had lined it with damp clay from the stream bed. He then dried it by the fire. Could this rock-hard basket be used to carry a small fire? It was awkward and heavy, and would need frequent addition of wood, but perhaps it would work. This was Eevo's hope. Use the basket to carry the fire to the home cave of the clan. After a permanent fire was established there, she could return to their own cave with a portion of that fire.

Eevo, even more than Sim, was extremely interested in fire. Where did it come from? What was it? She had tried putting various things on it to see what foods it liked. She did this when she first met fire that night outside the small cave and, since that time, continued to try different things. She knew that fire ate anything that grew and nothing that had not grown. It ate no earth, no rocks and no water. Water, in fact, fought the fire and, if there was more water than fire, the fire died. Moreover, the remaining wet wood would not light until the water was gone. If there was more fire than water, the mix of the two would crackle and spit until the fire drove the water away, and then it would become a normal fire. Where the water went to was another one of her puzzles.

Of all the things she fed the fire, dry wood seemed to be its favourite food, but a small fire could not eat a large piece of wood. One had to give it small pieces until it grew big. Then it could eat and be happy to eat even the biggest pieces of wood she could find. When the fire had finished eating, what was left was a grey powder that, as Sim had pointed out, was much like the brownish grey powder found around trees that had fallen a long time ago.

Could it be that fire lived in wood and in other things that grew? She knew that when she was out in the sunlight she felt warm, sometimes in the summer much too warm. Did the sun get into things when they grew? Things did grow quickly when there was more sunlight and the weather was warm. Did the sun put little bits of itself into growing things? Was fire really sunlight getting back out when the growing thing died? But when a stick was broken there never was any fire falling out. It was puzzling indeed.

One day, while looking at the fire, she remembered the time when she was working on the dry wood for the spears. When she had smoothed the shaft with a rubbing stone, the wood had become quite warm. This morning, while selecting a spear to give to Ab, she tried the rubbing again. Again the wood had become warm. Now, with the others gone, she was alone for the first time. She would try to release the fire from the wood. Eevo reasoned that, if, as she suspected, fire lived in the wood, rubbing might let some of the heat out.

If she rubbed one piece of wood with another, the heat coming out of both pieces might be enough to release the fire. Since water fought with the fire and drove it back into the wood, she would use some of the very dry wood from the tree that Sim used to make his good spear shafts. And, because a little fire could not eat a large piece of wood, she would use little thin pieces.

Eevo took a small flat piece of wood and put it on the dry ground close to the fire that always burned in the cave. Then, carefully selecting another small flat piece, she started to rub the first one with it. But this second one was too thin and it broke. She found another somewhat bigger round piece and started rubbing the one on the ground again. At first nothing much seemed to be happening. She stopped and felt the end of the rubbing piece. It was hot, much too hot to touch comfortably. Encouraged, she started again, rubbing faster and faster. By now her arms were aching, but she had managed to rub a little furrow into the flat piece of wood on the ground. And now this furrow was filling with a brownish powder and a few wisps of smoke were coming from it.

Eevo rubbed harder and faster. She was so excited that she forgot her aching arms, forgot the soreness of her knees on the rock floor, forgot everything except the increased smoke from the powder. Now there was the glow of an ember in the powder. She stopped rubbing and, controlling her breathing with effort, began to blow gently on the ember. A little flame burst out! Eevo carefully added small chips and shavings to this tiny flame and, as she knew how from her months of keeping the cave fire alight, built up her own, her newly-created fire.

A feeling of wonder passed through her and she knew that she had just done the most important thing in her life. Then, stopping for a while to look at it again, she got up and went to the cave entrance. She looked up to the sun and said, "Thank you for letting me release the bit of you that you put into all growing things. I will always give thanks to you for the warmth and safety that your fire gives. I will not let your secret be lost, but I will teach it to all the people I meet."

Eevo took the flat piece of wood she had first used and the rubbing stick and tried again. This time, knowing what to expect, it was easier. Putting her fire-making sticks into her neck pouch, she thought for a moment, then added another similar set. This was now a part of her person, to be with her always.

Inside were the original cave fire and the two fires that she had just made. Eevo had learned the secret of releasing the little bit of sun put into the wood when it was growing. She believed that after the fire was let out, the part that remained was like rock and earth. The living part that had been in the wood left and probably went back to the sun when the wood burned. There was so much about the sun that she did not understand. But she would learn as much as she could. Now that she knew how to get the sun part, the fire, from inside the wood, she had to teach all the people.

Eevo prepared kindling for another fire and waited for Sim.

All this had taken a fair amount of time and the day was almost past when she heard the wolves playing in the snow. On their heels came Sim with a large chunk of the elk meat and, better still, some fresh liver. The wolves had eaten well and now, coming into the warm cave, as usual when they had nothing they wanted to do, they lay down near the fire and went fast asleep. Sim wanted to tell Eevo about the elk and about the trip to the old home cave. Eevo wanted to talk about the fire. Both ended up talking at the same time.

Finally, Eevo said, "I'm hungry." Sim agreed that he was too. For the first time, he noticed that there were three fires burning and that there was kindling for another fire. He asked, "Why?" She told him she would show him while the meat he brought was roasting. They cut strips of fresh elk, skewered them on sticks and arranged them over the glowing coals.

Eevo then took the flat piece of wood and the rubbing stick out of her bag. She knelt and, placing the flat piece of wood on the ground, began to rub it with the rubbing stick. Sim wanted to ask questions, but Eevo was working too hard to answer. Finally, when a wisp of smoke arose from the brown powder that the rubbing had produced, Sim realized what she was doing and became very excited. At last, when Eevo had almost given up from fatigue, the powder glowed into a small ember and, with careful fanning from her hand, a flame was started which she transferred to the kindling. Soon there were four fires burning. Sim grabbed Eevo about the waist and hugged her so hard he almost knocked her down. Even the wolves woke, and not knowing what it was all about, joined in the great excitement.

"Now we can travel and go to look for Mother and

Father," exclaimed Sim.

"Yes, but first we must get ready for the trip. We also promised to take fire to the home cave and to teach some of the people there how to look after it," Eevo reminded him. "Anyway, it is not a good time to travel as yet. There is much snow. Besides, what shall we do with the wolves?"

"They will come with us," Sim replied.

"Of course," said Eevo, "on the trip, but what about at the home cave?"

"I don't really want to spend time in the home cave," stated Sim. "Outside of Ab and the two girls, Ur and Ree, who were your friends, no one liked me at all. When you were not around, especially when I was small, they teased me. They said I was lame and useless. After Mother and Father left, they drove me away and threw stones at me. You know all that."

"Yes." Eevo clearly remembered all that had happened. "But that was the best thing they did for both of us. If they had let us stay we would now be starving, just as they were before we sent them the food. Remember, there is Ab who was Father's favourite hunting companion, and those two girls."

"I know what to do," suggested Sim, "something that will solve all the problems. You are right. It's too early to start on such a long trip. The weather can become quite bad. The wolves and the people in the cave would not get along and I don't want to spend any time with most of the people. What we should do is bring the two girls to this cave. I am sure that Ur would be willing to come, she always liked to do unusual things. Ree would come if her friend was coming."

56

Checking to see if Eevo seemed to like his idea, Sim continued, "Once they're here, we could teach them how to take care of a fire. You could even teach them how to make a fire. If they become the ones in the cave who look after the fire, they would become important. Then no one would punish them again. Don't you think that they are the sort who would get along with the wolves?

Sim took a deep breath and looked at Eevo. But, before giving her a chance to answer, he had more to say, "As for Ab, he has always been our friend and he wants a fire to help protect the home cave. He is their most important hunter. Now that he knows that the big deer can be hunted, he can get lots of food for the people. He was very brave when the elk ran toward us. He was terrified and wanted to climb a tree, but I was standing there and he would not desert me. As scared as he was, he stayed and attacked that huge animal. I tell you, I was more than a little frightened myself when I saw how big that elk was. We need to help Ab. Besides, he may know the direction Mother and Father took."

Sim stopped and Eevo simply nodded her head in agreement. The thought that now they might be able to look for their parents was most exciting of all. Sim, not wanting to spend time in the old home cave, had settled the problem of how the clan would react to living with wolves.

Together, they began to make the necessary preparations. Strips of meat were set up to dry. During warm weather they would have done this in the sunlight, but as it was still winter they used their fire. Not knowing what hunting might be like on their trip, they needed to have supplies. The wolves, they knew, could look after themselves, but having extra food along would be a good idea.

There was nothing in which to carry water and so they did not even consider taking any. Sim worked at making extra spears and was busy breaking and chipping flint for spear heads and extra knives. He could get cutting edges, but he could not shape them. When he was lucky, he got something he could use, but each spearhead he made was different from any other. Not one, however, could match the good knife his father had.

Two days passed. About noon of the third day, the wolves momentarily lifted their heads and pricked their ears. Sim though he heard something. The wolves relaxed and settled back to doze, but Sim continued to sense something coming. Picking up the spear he kept beside him, he listened as the sound came closer. Why were the wolves not interested? When he saw Ab come into view, he understood. Of course, the wolves had recognized the scent of an accepted member of their pack. No wonder they went back to sleep. A relieved Sim greeted Ab and found that it was good to see another person.

"I came because I want to speak to you and Eevo," said Ab. "The people at the cave are happy about the food. But they are not ready to believe that you are alive. They are certainly not prepared to believe in helpful wolves. They even have difficulty in believing that I am not a spirit. The respect I get now is great but fearful. I don't know whether to like it or to worry about it. I don't know if it would be wise to have you come back to the cave. Having fire would be most helpful, but the people would be afraid of it. They wouldn't know how to take care of it."

Sim laughed. He told Ab that he and Eevo had similar thoughts. He also told him that now Eevo could make fire whenever she wanted to and that she even had a pretty good idea as to what fire was. Ab was startled. His idea that

58

perhaps the children and the wolves were not real but were spirits came back for a moment. Then he remembered the elk hunt. It was no spirit that thrust that spear into the elk, but a strong young arm attached to a strong young body.

Eevo came out and was very pleased to see Ab. He congratulated her at once on the fire-making, realizing what an important discovery it was for everyone. Sim told her that Ab had reached the same conclusion about their returning to the cave as they had. He also thought that it would be better if they and the wolves did not come.

Eevo described their idea to Ab. They would invite Ur and Ree to come and stay with them and learn about fire keeping. The two young women could then return to the home cave and be the "Keepers of the Fire."

Ab liked that plan. He told them that both girls had admired Shim. When she was at the cave, they had tried to imitate her. But, because there had been a somewhat hidden resentment of Shim, the two girls were now the brunt of the women's scorn. They were having a bad time. They were shouted at, given the worst work to do and frequently hit. When he, Ab, was there he tried to stop the abuse, but that only seemed to make matters worse. He felt that if Ur and Ree became the fire keepers, and he was sure that no one else would even try to learn how, the girls might not be better liked, but they certainly would become very important to the well-being of the group. They would become, as he had since his return, people whom no one would dare offend.

Ab offered to bring the girls to the cave, but was worried that their lack of travelling experience might put them in danger during such a long journey through dangerous country. Eevo agreed, thought a moment, and with a big grin on her face, made her suggestion. Two days from now, she, Sim, and the wolves would be waiting in the clump of trees near the home cave. They would be there at the time the sun was at its highest point in the sky. Ab was to talk to the two girls and tell them the plan. He was to do his best to convince the two that Eevo and Sim were alive and well and they were still their friends. He was to tell them all he had learned about the happenings after the clan had driven Sim away. Then, just before the sun was at its peak, he was to announce to all the people that Ree and Ur had been chosen to bring a bit of the sun into the cave. This bit of sun, called Fire, would keep the people warm in the cold. And most importantly, people would be safe, especially the little children. No predator would dare enter a cave where fire lived.

Ab would tell the people that Sim, Eevo and the wolves had come to take the young women back with them to their own cave. There they would discover how to tend and feed the fire. After they had learned, they would return and bring the fire with them, to live with the people of the cave. The fire keepers would stay and look after the fire as long as they received respect and proper treatment and a fair share of the food.

"When they see us and the wolves waiting in the grove among the trees, I'm sure that will impress the clan," said Eevo. "After all, they believe that we are spirits. When Ur and Ree go back, I'm sure that no one will think of hitting them again."

The thought of how the people would react had them all laughing. In the midst of the merriment, Sim became serious. He asked Ab if he knew where Mother's people lived, as Eevo and he wanted to go there to find their parents. Ab also stopped laughing and became very serious.

"It is very far. I know only the general direction. First you must climb through mountain country. Then there is a long stretch of sand with no water and few animals. It is a bad land to be lost in. I know how eager you are to find them. I tried to myself, but after going in the direction of the setting sun for as many days as I have fingers one one hand, and finding no sign of people, I turned back. I'll speak to the other hunters. Perhaps one has met someone who knows the way to Shim's people. But I would be happier if you did not try to go."

After having some of the meat that the fire had changed, which Ab now quite liked, he headed back toward his home cave. The wolves decided to accompany him for some way and he was grateful for their company. It was wonderful having such powerful friends. Then, thinking over the scheme that he and the others were planning, he began to chuckle to himself as he trudged home.

Seven

Ree and Ur

Eevo and Sim worked hard for the next two days. Despite the snow they went to the place where the rushes grew and cut enough for two beds. Firewood was gathered and piled neatly against the cave wall. Now, as before, only the one fire was providing heat. Over the flames, suspended in the smoke, strips of meat were curing. The smoke curled up and left the cave through the opening high up the wall. Extra clay mud from the bottom of the stream had been plastered over the bottom of the fire pot and it, too, was placed by the fire to dry.

Three skin cords made from deer hide were tied to the wicker frame of the fire pot. The other end of each cord was tied to the centre part of a pole, a somewhat crooked spear that Sim had discarded. This would be carried with one end on Eevo's shoulder and the other on Sim's. In that way, the pot dangled from the spear shaft and the person behind could keep an eye on the fire. By the end of the trip whether or not the fire pot worked would be known.

A good supply of wood was prepared with sticks being broken into short lengths to fit the fire pot. These were bundled into the wood-carrying skin, the one that had been used as a toboggan to bring Ab to the cave. Eevo made a little pad of rushes which she had covered with mud, and then dried and baked on the fire. This pad was to be a lid to cover the fire pot to slow down its flames, but still allow enough air to keep the fire from going out.

On the second morning, ignited wood from the home fire was transferred into the fire pot and covered with the lid. The wolves and Sim and Eevo began their trek to the home cave of the clan, a trip that did not take long now that they knew the way. They stopped in the trees, just a few hundred paces from the cave, but because of a small hill separating them from their former home, they knew they could not be seen. The sun was almost at its highest point. They waited.

Two days earlier, after the meeting with the children, Ab had returned to the home cave. After being greeted by the people, he was asked if his hunt had been successful. He told them that he had not been hunting, but had gone to speak with Sim and Eevo. Then, he looked for Ree and found her scraping the skin of the elk, working to remove all the fat and to soften the hide. He asked where Ur was.

"She's hauling up stones so the men and boys can practise throwing," said Ree. "She has been doing that all day without anything to eat. I hope they get tired soon. She looks exhausted."

"I will put a stop to that now," said Ab. He went to the stream where the men were and called, "Ur, stop what you are doing and come here to me."

One young man objected. "We need her to fetch us stones so that we can practise," he said.

"One of you can do that, or you can get one of the young boys to do so. I need both Ur and Ree for an important matter." Ab repeated, "Come with me," to Ur. Together, they returned to Ree.

Ab told both girls to sit down as he had something of great importance to discuss with them. "I need your help," he said, very seriously. The girls were amazed that an important hunter would want to talk to them. They were used to having people order them to do things, never ask. The only adult who had ever requested their opinion on anything had been Shim. Dedu had always been kind, but had almost never talked to them. Now the chief hunter was treating them as if they were important. They looked at each other in utter bewilderment.

Ree thought to herself, 'I have heard the men say that Ab has become strange, and some fear that it is not really Ab, but a spirit that has taken Ab's appearance.' A shiver went through her. 'But then, why would a spirit need our help?'

Ab began, "Listen carefully to what I tell you. Then, when I am finished, ask about anything you don't understand, and if I can, I will explain." He told them what had happened when Sim had been driven from the cave, the story of the fire, the hyenas, the cave, the wolves and his rescue. He continued with a detailed account of the trip back to the home cave and the killing of the elk that ended the people's starvation. That last part they knew.

The chief hunter told the girls how the sun had let Eevo

release fire from the wood and that, in the time the children had been away, they had grown to more than adult size. He felt that this was due to the sun, that the sun had taken the children under its protection and sent the fire to them, made them bigger, and removed their fears by sending the wolves as their helpers.

He told the two young women that Eevo had made a promise to the sun that she would teach its secret to all the people she met. All three, Sim, Eevo and Ab, thought that, for this group of people, it would be best to have Ree and Ur become the "Keepers of the Fire." They believed that Ree and Ur should be the chosen ones. But, since the work to be done was very demanding, the chosen people would have to be willing to devote their lives to this task. They would really have to want to do it. He then told them the difficulties of this work. As special people they would have responsibilities that other young women would not have. Some clan members might even fear them. He urged them to think about this possibility overnight and to discuss it between themselves. By midday tomorrow, Eevo, Sim and the wolves would be waiting for them in the treed grove over the small hill in front of the cave.

Ab wanted to give them the privacy they needed for something so important, so he sent them to his sleeping place in the cave, his private place where no one else was permitted. There, they could think and talk and not be bothered by anyone. He would sleep nearby and would hear their answer in the morning. If they agreed, he would tell the people. If they disagreed, he would have time to stop Eevo, Sim and the wolves.

The girls got little sleep that night. They talked, worried and hoped. But, having made their decision by morning, they told Ab, "Yes."

A short while later, Ab stood up in the entrance to the cave and announced, "I have a message for the whole clan." When the people had gathered, he started by saying, "This is a message from Sim, whom you drove out of the cave before the end of the time of the berries. It is also a message from Eevo, his sister. These two young people are alive. They survived because they are under the protection of the sun."

The people looked at one another and began to laugh. Ab was losing his mind again, talking about the dead as if he could speak with them. But even though they thought that he was mad, they still were just a little afraid of not listening.

Ab continued, "Eevo and Sim have asked Ur and Ree to live with them for a time. They will learn how to feed and take care of a piece of the sun. This is called Fire. This Fire has great power. It will keep the people warm even when snow is falling outside the cave. It will keep predators away. It gives light. It makes food softer and more tasty."

The people knew that all these were things were impossible, but Ab talked as if they were real. He kept on talking about two dead children as if they were alive and more powerful than a grown man. This was spirit talk, not to be believed. But then they remembered that Ab had brought food. He had come back from a hunt, after being lost by the rest of the hunters. He had carried a knife and was wearing very good skins sewn into clothing, clothing better than anyone had ever seen. Ab was also acting like a leader. The people of the cave responded to this new authority, even though they doubted much of what he said.

Ab told them that Eevo, Sim and the wolves would be coming to the home cave when the sun was at its highest.

They would take Ree and Ur with them. Once trained, the two young women would return with the fire, and would become the "Keepers of the Fire." The people would have the fire for as long as the young women were treated with the respect that a fire keeper deserved. They were to have a portion of food each, as much as the hunter who brought the food. If this was not done, the young women would leave the cave and the fire would go out and the sun would no longer protect these people.

Ab said all this in so firm a way that many of the people were afraid not to believe. Still some were not convinced. There was much discussion and no agreement. The morning passed.

Ab looked up to the sun and waited a few minutes longer. Then, as the sun appeared to be directly overhead, he did something strange. He raised both arms toward the noonday sun and held them that way for about as long as it takes to take ten breaths. Lowering his arms, he called to the girls, "Come with me." He walked toward the trees, with Ree and Ur on either side of him. The people watched all this from a safe distance, curious, fearful and skeptical.

As Ab and the girls reached the top of the rise, two large well-dressed people walked out from the clump of trees. They carried something on a stick between them. On either side of the two humans was a large wolf. The two humans put down what they were carrying and the taller of the two uncovered the object in the centre. Something was thrown into it. A puff of smoke followed by flames leaped into the air. Was this the Fire that Ab told them about?

The people stood, silent, in awe. As Ab and the two girls approached the strangers, the taller of the two ran towards them. Ree and Ur ran forward. With great joy, they hugged

68

each other. Amidst the sound of laughter, the wolves approached Ab and stood beside him while the second of the two humans, a man limping slightly, came closer, carrying two hunting sticks such as those Ab now used.

The people knew then that this was Sim, but a Sim who was taller than Ab, a big man by clan standards. If the other was Eevo, then she was taller than everyone. Were they real people or were they something else? What might they be? Everyone wondered, but no one was prepared to move closer. Nor did they care to go too close to the wolves. Then the Eevo-thing approached the group and spoke in a very Eevo-voice, "We will borrow Ur and Ree from you. When they come back, they will bring you Fire to protect and warm you. They will keep the Fire going for you and teach the secrets of Fire."

Turning back, she and Sim picked up the fire pot. Accompanied by Ree and Ur, and with the wolves as guides, they went off into the forest. Ab returned to the cave. No one laughed at him or threw funny glances at one another. Ab was the unchallenged leader of the clan.

Ur could scarcely believe what was happening. Yesterday she had been busy gathering stones so that the young men of the clan could practise their throwing. If they missed their target, she was blamed and shouted at for not bringing them good stones. Today, she was with old friends, friends she had thought dead. Not only were they alive, but they had become very special. And if Ab was correct, and there was no reason to doubt him, she and Ree would also become special people. The days of doing the worst jobs and of being everyone's slave were over.

But also, they were with wolves. Ab had said that the wolves were friends, but she had had doubts about that even if she believed everything else. But it all seemed to be true. She looked around her. Here she was, walking through the snow, predators were all around, out-of-sight, but there. And she felt safe. Ur looked at Ree and could read on her face that she was having similar thoughts. Just where they were going she knew only from Ab's story, but since everything he had said had happened, she was no longer afraid. It was wonderful to be outside and not in danger. It was even more wonderful to be away from the cave and all the bullying.

Ree had her own thoughts. She had been very young, just beginning to walk when Shim had come to the cave with Dedu. Shim was different from the other women. She laughed, and loved to run, and played with the children. Ree remembered a little doll made out of scraps of fur that Shim had made for her. It was the first toy she ever had. She remembered being taken for walks and her mother being angry for some unknown reason.

When she was bigger, another young one had joined her in coming to play with Shim. That was Ur. It was good being with Shim. She always had time to spend with them and often had something for them to eat. Sometimes she even made reed baskets for the two girls. And then, when Ree was about three years old, Shim gave birth to a daughter.

Ree's mother told her that now Shim would not have time for her because she would be busy with her own child. Ree remembered that, at first, she did not like this new baby. But Shim had told Ur and Ree to come as usual and that this was their baby, too. All three of them would look after this new little girl.

Since this was her baby too and, since the baby had not

spoiled her fun with Shim, the dislike disappeared and was replaced by affection. Next, Sim was born. Now there were the four to look after him, Shim and the three little girls. Ree glanced at Eevo walking along with the fire pot suspended on the spear between her and Sim. "How much like her mother she is," she thought. "Sim is too, but he is more like Dedu."

Ree continued her thoughts. She remembered Ab as he had been. He was one of the older boys of the clan. At the time Sim was born, he had seemed grown up to Ree, but was probably only five years older than she was. He too, liked to be with Shim and also with Dedu. Quieter than Shim, Dedu was an extremely kind man who never ordered anyone about, a very patient man who was willing to spend as much time as necessary teaching hunting skills to the young men and boys. His favourite pupil was Ab and Ab loved Dedu. Ab was the only one of the male members of the clan who was kind to Sim and also pleasant to the three girls.

Ab had never taken a mate. Ree was very glad about this, but felt that he could never be interested in someone like herself. Then, shaking her head to clear it of these thoughts, she looked about her and watched as the wolves ranged in front of them. Nothing escaped their attention.

The group moved out of the wooded area and on to an open plain, where patches of grass were showing here and there among the areas of drifted snow. The sun was going down, but twilight was lasting longer each day. For the first time, Ree saw a land with no trees. There was no protection, nothing but swiftness of foot. She knew that such areas were avoided by the hunters from the cave. She looked at Eevo who was completely unperturbed, as was Sim.

Eevo, catching her look, said, "Look ahead. See that cliff? At the base of it is the stream where we get our fish. Our cave is just this side of the stream. We'll soon be home. If our fire is still burning, it will be the longest it has gone without us to feed it. I hope it is. Then we will know that, if properly fed, fire can last all day. You see, we are still learning how fire behaves."

The party scrambled down a slope and soon the stream was in sight. On the right rose a cliff. All along its ledges large flocks of birds were gathering, returning as evening set in. As they came closer, Ree and Ur could see a small stream tumbling from the cliffside and an opening in the rock face just beyond it. The wolves raced ahead, stopped for some water and then disappeared inside the cave. Seeing the wolves drink, Ree realized how thirsty she was and asked, "Is it all right to go and have a drink?"

"Of course," said Sim, "but wait a little longer. It is easier to drink from the stream inside the cave."

Sim led them around a large black rock and the cave was there. It looked and smelled clean, not like the home cave. They walked in and Sim showed the girls the best place to drink. Meanwhile, Eevo went to the fire area. It was covered with grey ash and looked dead.

She took one of the sticks used for fire tending and began to brush the ashes aside. Just underneath the ashes were red embers that began to glow almost immediately as a fresh supply of air reached them. Once she added some wood shavings and small sticks, and blew gently on the embers, flames flickered up. With the addition of arm-sized sticks, the fire was soon its regular joyous self.

"If you build it up before leaving and then cover it so that only a little air gets to it, it seems it can go all day,"

72

said Eevo. "We will have to see if it can go through the night. I am getting a little tired of sleeping in turns, so that one of us can feed it in the night while the other sleeps."

"Let's find out. Let's have two fires, one that we feed as usual and the other that we cover with ash and stir up in the morning. Wouldn't it be good not have to go through the bother of lighting a new fire?" suggested Sim. "If it does work for two nights, then we can make it up in the evening. It would be great to have a good night's sleep."

"That's a wonderful thought," said Eevo. She and Sim put some meat on their green stick skewers and suspended the strips over the fire. Ree and Ur were aghast. The thought that their friends would burn good meat shocked them.

Sim, seeing their disapproving looks, explained. "Just wait for a bit and you will see why we do this. Of course, if you prefer your meat raw, you can have it that way. But I think that once you have tried the meat after the fire does what it does to it, you will like it our way."

While there was still enough light, Eevo took the two for a quick look around the outer parts and the area about the mouth of the cave. She pointed out the area that they used as a latrine and explained that by relieving themselves outside, they kept the cave clean and free from stink.

"We really learned this from the wolves," she said, and then added, "If you would like to wash, the water in the pond is not too cold."

The girls looked at her in astonishment. They did not know what she was talking about. Eevo suddenly realized that what she and Sim did regularly, ever since they discovered the pleasant sensation of being clean that first evening in the cave, was unknown at the home cave. She laughed and explained, "After we have eaten, Sim and I will show you what we do before we sleep. The wolves like it too. But let's check if the meat is done. See if you like it. Ab does. He always asks for some when he is here."

They returned to the fire to find Sim picking up a wad of greasy moss that he had placed under the roasting meat. The cooked flesh was now on a slab of wood in front of the fire, ready to be eaten.

The girls knew that the fire was the reason they were there, but they had never seen fire before that noon when it had flared up out of the fire pot, impressing both the people of the cave and the two new "Keepers of the Fire." They remembered hearing something about fire before, but in their minds they had pictured some terrible thing, something that frightened even the fiercest animals. Here in the cave, it was treated as another tool. Sim and Eevo warned them not to touch the glowing parts, not that they had any desire to get close to it. But to see the familiarity with which both Sim and Eevo treated the fire was surprising. If all the animals were afraid of it, why did the wolves not fear it? There they were, sleeping near the blazing wood.

The two newcomers sat down at a safe distance. When they picked up the strips of meat, Ree almost dropped hers. It was hot. Carefully, they each took a tiny bite, then another. Then, with a sigh of pleasure, each started in on the food as if they were starving. Actually, they were almost always hungry, but Eevo cautioned them not to eat too quickly. She suggested that they stop for some water from the spring.

Sim had prepared something special to celebrate the arrival of their friends. It was smoked fish. This gift, added to the welcome they were receiving, made both girls start to cry. Sim wondered what he had done to upset them, but Eevo understood and explained it to him. He said, "Of course, I understand. That is how I felt when you came with me when I was driven from the cave."

Once their emotions were under control, Ree and Ur were shown their beds and fur coverings. Eevo suggested that they would feel ever so much better after a wash. Sim said, "A wash all over would be better, but it is still too cold to really enjoy going into the pool." To the girls, washing seemed an unnatural thing to do, but even if strange it was fun. Soon there was a great deal of splashing and everyone was wet. As they sat drying by the fire, Sim remarked, "We could just as easily have had a bath."

Ree and Ur thought that they would be too excited to sleep, but the combination of little sleep the previous night, the wonderful supper and the washing, along with the warm glow of the fire, had them asleep in minutes. Sim and Eevo, grinning with happiness, watched them for a short time. Then, as it was Sim's turn to feed the fire, Eevo went to sleep. Sim would do so later.

The next morning, Ree and Ur started to fit into the routine life of the cave. But the freedom and the welcome caused teary eyes every so often. Gradually, the new situation began to seem normal. By the next day both Ree and Ur felt at home.

Then the lessons began. They learned what the fire liked to eat, that hard wood burns better and longer, that small pieces burn quickly but not for long, and that a small fire can not eat a large piece of wood. They were shown that dried grasses and leaves and wood scrapings burn very quickly and are required to start a fire from a small beginning such as an ember. They discovered that wet wood or green wood takes very long to start burning unless the fire is very big.

Ree and Ur learned quickly and were soon dependable fire-keepers. However, starting a fire by rubbing wood on wood was a skill that only Eevo had mastered. She could create a fire almost every try. Sim was successful about one time in four, but the girls, never.

Sim did not like failing so stopped trying. But the girls were there to learn. They had to keep at it. Sim, a watch-to-learn person, tried to see what the difference was between what Eevo did and the others did. There must be something different. It seemed that, although the others pressed as hard as Eevo and rubbed as fast, they would get the powder buildup but no smoke. When he was alone, Sim began to experiment away from the eyes of the others.

The times he succeeded in making fire occurred when he moved the rubbing stick back and forth only a very short distance. When he moved it farther there was no smoke, or very little, and there was no ember. He tried the two methods, moving the rubbing stick only a small distance and moving it with longer strokes, a longer distance. After each trial he touched the end of the stick. In each case it was hot, but far hotter if the distance it travelled while being rubbed was shorter. Sim now tried to make this distance as short as possible.

He put the end of the rubbing stick against the flat piece of wood and started spinning it between his hands. The heap of rubbed powder grew more quickly. Soon there was smoke and then a glowing ember. As his sister had done the first time, he repeated the process and, for once, was successful twice in a row.

Sim picked up his fire-making equipment and went into the cave where the others were. The way he walked and the big grin on his face caught Eevo's attention. She said, "What have you discovered, Sim? I know that look!"

"I think I have found why you are successful and Ur and

Ree are not. It has to do with how far you move the rubbing stick. Let me show you. If it works again you can try."

Sim put the flat slab of wood down, and began to twirl the rubbing stick between his hands. In a remarkably short time, the pile of powder that the twirling had produced began to smoke. Then came the ember. He did not bother lighting a fire but passed the equipment to Ree. She positioned herself as he had and, after two false starts when the rubbing stick slipped from between her hands, she started it twirling.

The powder heaped up and the wonderful smoke rose. Eevo was prepared. She put the bunch of dried leaves, grasses, and wood shavings down for Ree and she lit her first fire. Ur followed the same procedure and she too, created fire. The fire-making problem had been solved! The two girls swarmed over Sim, hugging him with excitement. To his amazement, he found that he liked the feeling.

Ur and Ree had been at the cave for more than a moon. They could handle the fire making and the fire keeping as well as Sim, and almost as well as Eevo. Soon the time was coming for them to leave, not something they really wished to do. Life with Sim and Eevo was so pleasant and so relaxed. The wolves had accepted them completely and both Ur and Ree thought nothing of going out to gather wood or eggs, always with an extremely able protector. Not only had they learned about fire, but they had made important contributions to the cave life.

Ur had watched that first evening when Sim gathered the fat drippings from the meat that had dropped on some moss. She remembered him throwing the moss into the fire. That moss had flared up quickly and burned for some time with a white flame that lit the entire cave. For the next few

days she had gathered as much of the liquid fat as she could and, since there were no containers to keep it in, she had used the baked clay lid of the fire pot.

One evening as they were about to eat, she, now unafraid of the fire, had picked up a burning stick. After placing a small amount of moss in the fat, lit the moss wick. It caught fire. The fat burned with such a steady white light that it seemed as if daylight were inside the cave. They could see things in the cave they had not seen before. The primitive lamp burned all evening. Of course, Sim had to see if it could be improved and he did make some changes, but the lamp was Ur's invention.

Ree, watching Eevo rubbing down one of the spears, had remarked, "Eevo, you throw stones better than anyone else. Why don't you throw a spear when you're hunting?"

When Eevo mentioned this to Sim, he thought it was a great idea. He chose some spears with fire-hardened points because flint is brittle and would shatter on impact with stone or hard ground. All four spent the afternoon practising the throwing of spears. Not only did they find it not too difficult, but they discovered that a spear was a weapon that could be very effective from as far away as ten paces. From that time on the four of them practised part of every day.

Ab had been to visit twice and saw how happy and increasingly attractive the two girls had become. They had also grown taller. He took this to mean that the sun had accepted them and had taken them under its protection. Ab now believed that the sun was the force that was responsible for all life.

Eight

Tiger

Living together had been a more than just pleasant. Even the work was fun. Regrettably, however, this time was about to end. Ree and Ur must return to take up the duties for which they had been trained. Even though parting was necessary, not one of them liked the idea. All sorts of reasons were found to postpone the departure as long as possible, but it could not be put off any longer.

As they were making preparations to leave, they saw Ab approaching, obviously upset. They knew from his appearance that something terrible had happened. The news he brought was frightening. A new predator had arrived, one that the people could not fight. A male sabre-toothed tiger had moved in close to the home cave. At first it had hunted elk, but the other day it had come right into the cave, killed one of the young boys and carried him off! The people were terrified!

The hunters had thrown stones and made as much noise as they could, hoping to drive it away, but they were helpless. They had only irritated it. The tiger had dropped the boy's body and snarled ferociously, driving all of the people back into their cave. It then picked up the body and left. Now that the tiger knew where the people lived, it could come back whenever it wanted to feed. The only solution Ab could think of was to leave the cave and look for a new home. But that would do nothing to stop the tiger from following.

"Do you know where his den is?" asked Eevo.

"We think it is in a small cave about two or three hundred paces from the home cave," said Ab. "Keeping a fire at the mouth of the home cave might stop it from coming in, but it can pick off anyone who leaves the protection of the fire. I don't know what to do. Even your sharp spears would not stop it, at any rate not before it killed some of the hunters brave enough to go after him. I really don't think too many would dare."

Ab, sank down on the ground exhausted.

Eevo turned to Sim. "Remember the hyenas? Remember what the grass fire did? It is still early in the day. We will take the fire pot. Ur, get all the melted fat we have, plus any other fat. We must start for the clan cave at once, before the tiger kills again."

Looking directly at Ab, she continued, "Have some food while we get ready. As we go along I will explain what we hope to do. I think it will work. Sim, you tie all the spare spears into the wood-carrying skin, all of them, the fire-hardened ones as well as flint-pointed. Put in a good supply of moss as well."

Ab felt a load lifting off his shoulders, the others were sharing his responsibility. Eevo's words stirred a long-forgotten, but powerful memory. "Ab, as we go along I will explain what we hope to do." He could almost hear Shim, Eevo's mother, saying the same words to him many years ago. At that time he was two or three years younger than Sim was now. Shim, Dedu and Ab had been at the mouth of the cave where Dedu was showing him the best way to wield a club. Shim was curing a skin, from the antelope carcass Dedu had stolen from a group of hyenas.

Then came the scream. Dedu grabbed his club and ran toward the sound, as did Ab. Fast as they were, Shim was faster. Zo, one of the women of the clan had found herself being surrounded by hyenas. She was carrying her little daughter who had just begun to walk. As yet, Zo had not been attacked, but the hyenas were circling her. In her panic, she had dropped her child. But before any hyena could snatch the child, a number of well-aimed stones struck them. Distracted, the hyenas saw a large man carrying a club and a smaller "two-legged" one running toward them.

The stone thrower ran to the child and scooped her up. With so many people threatening them, the hyenas retreated. As the mother reached for her crying baby, Shim said, "Let me hold her. Her arm is broken." Zo began to wail. Her little daughter was precious, but now with a broken arm she would have to be put out of the clan.

Almost immediately Dedu and Ab arrived. Shim asked Dedu to make sure the hyenas had really left and told Ab to sit down on a rock. He was to hold the child carefully. "Don't let her broken arm move," she said. "Put your hand underneath her arm and hold her gently on your lap. As we go along I will explain what we hope to do."

Turning to the frightened Zo, Shim said, "The little one's forearm is broken, but I think that I can fix it. The medicine woman of my people taught me how, but I will need help from you. Go to the mouth of the cave. There you will see the skin I was curing. Bring it to me."

Zo did as she was asked.

Shim gave instructions. She told Zo to sit beside her child, and to stroke her head and make comforting sounds. She told Ab to continue supporting the broken arm with his right hand. He was to place his left arm around the little girl to keep her secure. She then told Dedu to take the child's hand in his. While Shim helped support the place where the break was, he was to pull gently but firmly.

She warned Zo that this would hurt and she also told the child, who astonished her by nodding. Dedu, who was very strong but also very gentle, increased the force of his pull very slowly. The arm straightened and, as it got to the right length, Shim gave it a sudden bend the other way. There was a sharp crack and a gasp but no crying from the little girl.

"It's all done." smiled Shim. "Just hold everything as it is. There will be no more pain."

Shim took the flint knife from Dedu's pouch and sliced the antelope skin that Zo had brought. She wrapped the moist skin about the forearm and molded it to fit snugly. Then, telling Dedu to relax his hold slowly, she took the arm, bent it at the elbow, and continued to wrap it with the skin so that the elbow was bent in a comfortable position. Next, she took some cedar bark fibres and tied them around the hide bandage to keep it from slipping, and made a sling about the little girl's neck to hold the arm at rest.

84

"The hide will dry hard and hold the bones firmly. That will let the break heal," she told Zo. "I would like to see her every day until the arm is well. Does she have a name?"

"Her name is Ree," said Zo.

Now, so many years later, Eevo was using the same words. Ab felt that she knew what to do as well as her mother had. Now he had hope that they might beat the sabre-tooth tiger. He glanced at Ree and wondered if she remembered her first meeting with Shim.

The wolves sensed that all was not well. There was a strong odour of fear and anger in the air. Going over to them, Eevo put an arm around each neck and said, "We are going into danger. You have always been good faithful friends, but this is not your quarrel. Our opponent is too strong for you, I do not want you hurt, so go back to your people."

The wolves acted as if they understood and their response seemed to say, "The quarrel is one between our pack and another pack. We stay with our pack; now lead the way."

Gathering their equipment, the war party moved swiftly toward the clan cave. With four people who understood fire, the fire pot was tended on the go. With everyone in the party in excellent physical condition and the snow gone, the cave was reached in just a few hours. The wolves, smelling the air, picked up the scent of the tiger. Their hackles rose and their teeth bared. They knew the scent to be that of one of their enemies. The wolves were ready for a fight.

This time with no stopping at the clump of trees, they all moved straight toward the mouth of the home cave. There the clan hunters and the larger boys were standing behind piles of throwing stones.

"I wonder who gathered those," thought Ur. Then, seeing Ruf, the young man who had liked tormenting her, she said, "You, go and bring as much dry wood as you can carry and bring it here. We will need it to stop the tiger."

Ruf gasped and raised his arm, as he had in the past, intending to hit her. A growl from one of the wolves brought about a rapid change of mind. Ab repeated Ur's order. "All of you gather as much wood as possible. Your stones won't stop the tiger, the fires will."

Eevo, Ur, Ree and Sim spread out in front of the cave. Using the wood they had carried with them, they created a semi-circle of six piles of kindling just outside the entrance to the cave. Each pile was lit by the burning sticks from the fire pot. In a very short time all six small fires were flaming. As more dry wood and twigs were brought, each fire became a massive barrier of scorching heat. The cave was now secure. The people of the cave watched spellbound as they began to realize the power of fire.

Og came up to Ur and said, "I know you and Ree are real people, but I don't know about the others. They are different. Thank you for coming back into danger when you didn't have to. And thank you for bringing the one weapon which I now know will stop any animal. I have never spoken to a woman as I would to a man, but you and Ree are as brave as any man, braver than most. If we win in this fight with the tiger and, if neither of us is killed, may I be your friend?"

"Thank you," said Ur. "Having friends is good and I would like that. But now we must keep our fires going. We'll see if Eevo's plan to drive the tiger away will work."

"How do you plan to drive away an animal as fierce as a sabre-toothed tiger?" said Og. "I had not thought that far ahead."

"Eevo has a plan. It is much like the way they drove off the hyenas that were hunting them. It has to do with fire. Sim is getting things ready."

Og looked over to see Sim wrapping bundles of moss around the top end of a spear shaft. He had finished three and was making more. The spears were not the sharp flint tipped ones but those with fire-hardened points.

Sim explained to Og, "These are to set the tiger on fire. It's too dangerous to try to get to it in its lair. But, if we can lure it down here into the lower land where there's a lot of dried grass and shrubs from last year, we'll get it. Ree, Ur, Eevo and I have spent much time practising spear throwing. We'll get as close to it as possible, then throw these burning spears at it and into the grass. If that works, I think we'll see the last of this tiger. You and Ab have had no practice in spear throwing, but you can set the grass and bushes on fire using one of these burning spears."

Sim took a skin sack that had a thick liquid in it and poured some onto each bunch of moss. He picked up his spears and said, "It's time to call on the tiger."

Sim, Eevo, Ree, Ur and Ab, carrying their weapons and accompanied by the wolves, left the cave now protected by its ring of fire, and headed for the tiger's den. Og, seeing Ur with a spear and a burning branch like the others, also took a spear with a moss ball and joined them. The remaining hunters and young men stayed behind. Ab stopped momentarily to raise his arms to the sun as he had done when the two young women had first left the cave, then the group moved cautiously up the slope to the tiger's lair.

Each one carried a bundle of firewood. They made a line of these bundles, set them on fire, and stood, one behind each fire. Eevo started shouting and throwing stones into the den. The others joined in the noise and the wolves started to howl.

The tiger woke. Stones were flying into its den. Some hit its body, and hurt. The air was full of smoke. Wolves, enemies of the tiger, were howling out there. With a defiant roar, the tiger leaped out of the cave only to find the side of the hill covered with smoke and fire. To escape, it raced down the slope, keeping clear of the flames. Even the cave of the two-legged was burning, offering no safe place for the fleeing beast. It paused, and suddenly was attacked by the wolves. Ordinarily, a tiger could deal with wolves, but this was not an ordinary situation.

The tiger fled down the hill into the bushes at the bottom, the wolves nipping at its heels, only to be

struck by a hail of burning sticks. Immediately, all the grass and bushes around burst into flames. There was no safety here either. Aware of the danger it was in, the tiger had to find another escape. Seeing a gap in the line of fires on the slope, it ran toward the opening. But there was a small two-legged one in its way. This was Ur, armed and ready. With its jaws open, the massive tiger sprang at the seemingly vulnerable human. Suddenly, fire was in its mouth, burning its whiskers and its eyes. The tiger tore at the flaming stick with its paws, then turned and fled up the slope, running into rocks and stumbling into gullies. Finally, it was clear of the searing flames. Burned, almost blind and unable to smell, the tiger put as much space as it could between itself and that terrible valley.

A rousing cheer erupted from the onlookers. Og and Ab picked up Ur and carried her on their shoulders down to the cave. Everyone wanted to touch her and Ree. These were their own, their "Keepers of the Fire." Eevo, Sim and the wolves were respected, but somehow they were no longer cave people. They were more like spirits to be honoured.

Later, after the celebration of the defeat of the sabre-toothed tiger, Sim talked to the other hunters. But no one knew the way to Mother's people, just that it lay toward the setting sun. Only Ab had travelled any distance in that direction and he warned them again that there was very little game for food and even less water. Once more he advised against going. Sim and Eevo, however, had a mission; they had to find their parents.

Turning towards their own cave in the direction of the setting sun, they left the clan cave under very different circumstances than they had ten moons earlier. Along with the wolves, they were about to prepare for a long and dangerous journey.

Nine

Fire Not Ours

On the trip back home Eevo and Sim were silent. Each was engaged in private thoughts. They were beginning to realize the magnitude of what they had just accomplished. Without any injuries to themselves or the others with them, they had overcome one of the giant cats, the fierce sabre-toothed tiger that considered everything, no matter how large, as prey. Little did they know exactly how much they had changed. But they knew that, although their people respected them, they no longer felt like members of the home clan. They had become outsiders.

Eevo and Sim had rushed into terrible danger to help their clan, but they had gone as strong people from the outside coming to the aid of a weaker group. Now they were returning to their own home, having been successful in banishing the tiger. They had armed the clan with fire. They had provided the hunters with spears, giving them a better way to feed the people. All this was good, but they now knew that the clan cave was no longer their home. Somewhere in the direction of the setting sun were Mother and Father. Now finally, they were free to go out to look for them. But where to look? Would they ever find them?

They reached their cave as the sun was setting. Their great speed in leaving that morning meant they had, for the first time, neglected the fire. As well, they had left the fire pot with Ur and Ree. Their fire was out. While Sim prepared some kindling, Eevo made a new one. By now, the use of the fire sticks was a simple task. But despite the large fire they built, there was an emptiness in the cave, a loneliness without the sounds of other people. Ur, Ree and Ab would all be busy back at their cave. The wolves were good friends, but somehow it was not the same as with other people.

Sim and Eevo sat by the fire and warmed themselves, ate some of their dried smoked meat, and began to talk about tomorrow. Were they really ready to start out on their search? Should they wait a few days? They had learned how to be independent. They could make their crude but useful flint tools. They had learned how to live and cooperate with wolves and had learned how to make fire. They were now the hunters, not the hunted. Fear was no longer part of every day. They were still very young, but they had become strong capable people, here in this cave, their home. Now they were planning to leave it.

Deep in thought, they looked at their surroundings. Sim broke the silence. "Eevo, the sun is almost set. Let's go out and climb to the cliff top. We have never gone out when darkness was beginning, the time when the wolves like to go out. Why should we stay in our cave? We have fought the hyenas and now they stay away from us. And today we drove off a tiger! Let's each take a spear and go out. We've never seen the outside at night except when we first met fire at the small cave. That fire made it light for us."

Eevo looked at him and said, "You know it is something not done, not ever. But I've always wanted to." She jumped to her feet and said, "Let's go!" The wolves, sensing the excitement, got up too. All four stepped out into the night, sniffed the air for the scent of any predators, then climbed the path they knew so well from their egg hunting expeditions.

From the top of the cliff they looked over the valley below. The last glow of the sun was still visible, but the sky was filled with many points of light which looked cold and far, far away. Sim and Eevo stood and gazed with wonder! What were these? They were never seen in the daytime. As they scanned the sky, low on the horizon they saw another light, different from the lights in the sky. This light was a warm yellowish-red glow, like the light of their fire. They stared at it for some time. Eevo, reaching over, touched Sim and said in a quiet, almost frightened voice, "Fire, but not ours. It is not a grass fire, as it is not growing. It must be a people fire, but whose?"

They noted its direction. Tomorrow that was where they were heading!

Early next morning they climbed to the cliff top again and stared in the direction of last night's fire. Nothing was to be seen. Had they really seen a fire? They looked carefully at the land in the distance. There was a small range of hills rising from the open grassland, the type of country without trees for shelter that humans had always feared. But no longer were Eevo and Sim held back by such thoughts of danger. They were the beginning of a new breed of people. For them, the open grassland was a place to hunt.

With two spears each and some dried meat in their carrying pouches, they set out. While Sim's limping gait allowed him to move quite quickly, the wolves and Eevo adjusted their pace to his. Before the sun had reached its high point, they could make out the details of the line of hills they had seen from the top of the cliff.

Suddenly the wolves pricked up their ears. Something was ahead. With Eevo taking control as pack leader, they

moved forward more slowly and cautiously. Just a few hundred paces before them they saw two people, one tall and slender, the other heavier and powerful looking. The slender one was carrying a container that gave off bits of smoke. She put it down, then stood up and pulled loose a spear that had been strapped on her back.

The heavy-set one was carrying a spear, with another on his back. They eyed Eevo and Sim and especially the two wolves. The two sides approached one another with care. The slender one suddenly stopped and stared at Sim.

"Sim," she called, "can that be you? Why are there wolves about you? Is that you, Eevo? What are you doing out here?"

"Mother!" Eevo cried. "It's really you and Father!" As the two women ran to reach other, the wolves ran forward as if to protect Eevo. Sim called and signalled them to stop. They did, but remained on guard in case these strangers should be hostile. Tearfully, Sim ran with his rolling gait toward Dedu. The two men stopped and looked at one another. Both were of similar height, one slender and beardless, obviously young, and the other bearded, heavy-set and very strong.

"Have we been away that long?" exclaimed Father. "You are as tall as I am! Eevo is taller than her mother! Is time different in different places? I thought that we had been away for 10 or 11 moons. But both of you must be full grown. And the wolves! Tell me about the wolves. I can see that they are your friends, but how is that possible? I have always respected wolves, but never did I think that they could become friends."

"Father," replied Sim, "I want to hug Mother. Then let's hurry to our cave. We no longer live with the clan. At our cave we can eat and tell you our story and you will tell us yours." He hugged his mother as Eevo came to Father.

In the midst of the excitement, Shim remembered, "Wait a moment. I must pick up my container of fire. It carries one of the most wonderful things in this world. It makes people safe from the night hunters."

"I know," said Sim. "Come, let's hurry back. We have much to hear and much to show you and much to tell you."

Father had noticed the spears Eevo was holding. He

reached over and touched one, looked at the sharp flint point and asked, "Where did you get these?"

"Sim made them," said Eevo proudly. "He has also made flint knives. They're good, but not as good as your old knife."

Father just stared. "Sim makes things from flint?"

"Yes, Father. Here's the knife he made for me."

Father turned to Shim. "Did you hear that?" he asked. "Sim must meet your father. He is exactly what your father hoped to find."

He continued, "Sim, when Mother mentioned the wonderful fire, you answered, 'I know.' How can you know?"

Sim told Father that they knew about fire, but it was a long story. They would tell it as soon as they were home. He also said that they had a fire in their cave.

"But it will go out if you do not keep it fed," said Mother. "That would be terrible. It is good that we met you today so that I can give you some if yours is out. But, why are you out in this dangerous grassland?"

"We were looking for the fire we saw last night," said Eevo.

Sim interrupted, "Eevo, Mother and Father must be tired from their long trip. Ab told us how hard it was when he tried to find them. Let's hurry home."

Mother agreed, and went back to get her fire carrier. "We must get some wood along the way."

Eevo, the practical one, asked, "Have you eaten today? You have been on a long journey."

"We found some roots last evening," Mother replied,

"but we are hungry."

"Then, let's have some food before we start back. While you eat we can tell you a little of why we are no longer at the home cave and how the wolves joined us. The wolves live with us. They're part of our family."

"A good idea," answered Mother, astonished at the suggestion. "But I don't know what we can find to eat."

"We have some meat with us." And Eevo gave them some strips of smoked meat out of her neck pouch. Mother felt the meat, then smelled it and took a bite.

"What have you done with this? What kind of animal does it come from?" she asked.

"It tastes very good," said Father. "I"ve never had anything quite like it."

"It's the meat of one of the elk from the herd that grazes near the home cave. Sim and Ab and the wolves killed one at the end of the cold time. We dried and smoked the meat," said Eevo.

Father looked at Sim with admiration. "There is much that I have to learn about my son," he said.

"And your daughter, too!" added Sim.

While they were eating, Sim began to talk, "Before we start heading home, I would like you to meet our friends, the wolves. Let me call them so that they can get your smell and recognize you from now on."

The wolves came over when called and sniffed around Father and Mother. While checking out Mother, they went from her to Eevo and then back, and repeated this a number of times. They appeared just a little confused and, on the trip home every so often would actually brush against Shim as they liked to do with Eevo. When one did so, she would rub its neck or head. Mother, after watching this, did the same. Although the wolves shied away from her at first, by the time they arrived at the cave they seemed quite happy to have two-neck rubbers who looked and even smelled very much alike.

Once inside the cave, Mother and Father looked around and were amazed. Giving each other quizzical looks, they sat down on the rush beds while Sim and Eevo continued to tell their story.

"Ab allowed this to happen?" interrupted Father in an angry voice.

"He had no choice," explained Eevo. "He had been badly hurt the day after you left, as had Ro. They were not able to do anything. But I am glad that Sim was put out and I left. Had we stayed, we might have starved. No babies survived the cold time and the whole group almost died because of no food."

The story of their first night, the little cave, the storm and what they had called "the tree eating animal," their study of fire, the defeat of the hyena pack, the new cave and how they got the wolves, all this was told. Throughout, Father and Mother asked questions. Finally Eevo and Sim brought out more food. They ate and continued their story.

Both parents were astounded. How could their young children have done so much? But Mother had one concern.

"You left the fire in the cave this morning and did not take any with you. What would you have done if the fire went out?"

"Eevo or I would have started a fresh one," Sim said.

Mother and Father stared at him. "How?" they both said.

"I'll show you," Sim said.

"No, I will," said Eevo. Reaching into her bag, she took out her fire-making tools. She prepared some kindling and, kneeling on the ground, proceeded to start a new fire under the wondering gaze of both parents and the proud smile of her brother.

"This is the most important thing of all," said Father. "This makes it possible for people to travel where they want. This skill must be shared with others. We must go back to your people, Shim, and give them this wonderful gift. They deserve it for all they did for us and the things they, especially your father, taught us. Things, it seems, our children found out for themselves. Eevo and Sim, go on with your story."

The rest of the story was told, the rescue of Ab, the starvation at the home cave, the elk that fed all the people for the rest of the cold time, Ur and Ree as "Keepers of the Fire," and how six of them went to war and how they drove off the sabre-toothed tiger. They had just returned to the cave last night to prepare for their trip to find their parents. That same night in their saying farewell to their familiar home, they had seen the fire that had led to the family being reunited.

Their parents were very impressed and very proud.

"You helped the people who tried to harm you and at very great danger to yourselves. Now that I know that you are safe, I know it's wonderful but maybe foolish, then again maybe not," concluded Mother.

Father just grinned with happiness and pride.

100

Next Father and Mother described their journey of ten moons ago. The first two days were uneventful, until they found themselves in a land of sand. The sun was far too hot for travel in the daytime. They continued to travel by night. This time, with Father along, she could enjoy the lights in the sky and the moon that lit their way,not like the time she had been lost, and then found by father.

Fortunately, Mother had remembered how her people got water from some of the plants growing in the sand country. After two nights of desert travel, they could smell water. Just ahead was a small oasis with a spring, where they were even able to kill a large water bird for food.

Two days later, they met a hunting group. Mother spoke to them and found that her father was alive but now an old man. He was still making spearheads and knives from flint, but was complaining that he had trouble seeing close-up. His knives and spears, while still good, were taking far longer to shape.

Mother had disappeared so long ago that she was believed to be dead. When the hunting group returned with the two travellers, her father could hardly believe his eyes. Her return, a reminder of times long past, almost made him feel young again.

Seer, Mother's father, was a clever man. He was the tool maker for the whole clan, a much larger group of people than those of Father's clan. The hunting ground of Mother's people included a large wetland where there were always many water birds, and even giant beaver. Here, hunting was not so dangerous. With plenty of fish and clams available, as well as tuberous plants of many kinds, mother's people were always well-fed. Father, although stronger than many of the men there, found himself to be among the shortest in height. This part he did not like. But he did enjoy hunting, especially for the geese that would come to the wetlands in great numbers. Not being hungry most of the time was a new experience for Father.

Seer was happy to make a knife for Father and one for Mother, along with some scrapers to make the dressing of skins easier. A good craftsman, he insisted that only a certain type of flint be used, but finding the right kind took time. Then, as he had told them, he had difficulty with close vision. He could not see just where to break the flint along its line of cleavage to get a long straight edge unless the light was bright and fell at just the right angle.

He was happy to have his daughter back and to have someone new to talk to, someone with whom to compare things. Seer thought a lot about many things. One of the things that bothered him a good deal was that young people tended to be lazy and without much ambition. They did not seem to want to learn and he could find no one whom he could teach the art of making good flint tools. He feared that with his failing vision soon there would be no one to provide the clan with good hunting tools. Things were not the way they had been when he was a boy. Then, children respected their elders and worked hard. Things were not as easy then as they were now. Now the young people were only interested in going out to hunt.

"I told my father about you, Eevo and Sim. I told him about your lame left foot, Sim, and how the people of the clan wanted you disposed of when you were a baby," Mother said.

Seer did not agree with that behaviour. In his opinion someone who is lame frequently is capable of learning useful skills. Father agreed that in an advanced society like

Seer's that was true, but in the more simple society of his cave clan there was nothing but hunting.

"If they had better hunting tools, your clan would improve," explained Seer. "As long as they don't have proper tools they can't advance."

"How can they get tools?" asked Father.

"Send the boy to me," said Seer. "If he is as bright as you say, and is willing to learn, I will teach him what I know."

Making the new knives and scrapers took longer than expected. Soon it was too late in the year to start the trip back and Mother and Father had to wait for the warmer weather. Finally, after reassuring Seer that they would be back with Sim and Eevo, they had started home. The trip back took as long in days as there are fingers on both hands because they were carrying that precious tool, fire, back with them. It needed much care to keep it going on such a long trip, but it did make the nights more comfortable and safe. No longer was there a need to spend night time in the trees.

Now, having returned with fire, they discovered that their children were at a more advanced stage in fire keeping than they were. A new fire could be made whenever needed ever since Eevo had reasoned things out. Sim had learned how to make flint tools. He had much to learn as yet, but on his own he had begun to shape flint the way he wanted it. With no instruction he had made spears, good ones too. He had improved the fire making, making it easier for many people to learn how. The two had adopted wolf cubs and turned them into friends, helpers on the hunt and protectors.

'Yes,' thought Father, 'It will be good to return to Mother's people and her father Seer, but not for a while. Perhaps we will go in the cooler weather when the leaves are beginning to fall.' He would ask Sim if he could think of a way to carry water. That would help on crossing the hot sands. Tomorrow he might go to the clan cave and see Ab and the others. Shim would probably like to see Ur and Ree. It was good to be home.

More About Cro-Magnon and Neanderthal People

At the time of this story there were two types of people living in the world. In this book we meet only the people, named Cro-Magnon because they or rather fossils of their skeletons were discovered in caves near the district of Cro-Magnon in France. The skeleton structure is the same as ours. These people were our ancestors. Because they were "Us," they were given the scientific name of Homo sapiens sapiens which means "wise wise man."

The other type of people who were living at that time were given the name Neanderthal because their fossil skeletons were found in the Neander Valley in Germany. Their skeleton structure is of a shorter heavier-boned people who had a more sloped and lower forehead than we do. They also had bony protective ridges above their eyes. Their brains were as large or slightly larger than ours. Because they looked so different from us, even though they certainly were people, the scientists who named them felt that they were more animal-like. These people were given the name Homo sapiens or "wise man." This group of people is now extinct and no one knows exactly how they lived or what destroyed them. People now like to think that we are the superior group. Sometimes the "label" Neanderthal is used to describe people who are not liked or whose behaviour is not appropriate. However, we do know that the Neanderthal buried their dead and, in some cases, the body for burial was wrapped in flowers, hardly the actions of an uncouth or brutish people.

Glossary

Alpha animal: In the structure of a wolf pack there is always a dominant animal to whom the others defer and obey. This leader may be male or female and sometimes both the dominant male and his mate will both be alpha animals.

Clay: Clay is a type of soil that is plastic-like and slippery when wet and completely impervious to water. It is used to make bricks and pottery and when dried and baked it is almost indestructible.

Elk: The elk is the largest member of the deer family and is called Moose in North America.

Ember: A burning glowing (but not flaming) coal or piece of fire, whether of wood, charcoal or coal is called an ember.

Entrails: This is the name for the contents of the abdomen of any animal. These contents would include the intestines, kidneys, etc.

Extinct: An animal or plant that is no longer living anywhere, is extinct.

Flint: Flint is a hard brittle grey quartz rock that breaks the way glass does, leaving razor sharp shards that can be used for cutting or piercing.

Gut: Gut refers to the fibrous part of the small intestine, commonly used as a cord for tying or sewing. Even now "cat gut" is used in surgery. It does not come from cats, but is usually from lamb gut.

Hyena: The striped hyena of north-east Africa and Asia Minor extending into the Caucasus mountains is the hyena of this story. This hyena is now an endangered species with only a small number left. A hyena weighs about 30 kilo, or 66 pounds, the size of a large dog. This is not the large spotted hyena (70 kilo) of the South Sahara region.

Instinct: An action that is born in every individual or member of a species is an instinct. Tail wagging in dogs is an example of an instinct. Dogs do not learn how to wag a tail after they are born.

Knapper: A Knapper is a person who is an expert in making flint tools.

Regurgitate: To regurgitate is to bring up previously chewed and swallowed food. Another word is vomit. A number of mammals and birds do this to feed their young.

Rushes: These are long grasses with a solid core. They would have been the predominant long grass growing in the marshes near the Old Clan area.

Sabre-toothed Tiger: This was a large, now extinct, car- nivore or meat eater, characterized by three to four-inch- long upper canine teeth. It was neither tiger nor lion but was of similar size. It preyed on all the larger herbivores or grass eaters.

Wolf: In this story, the largest of the wolves would have weighed 60 to 80 kilo (about 120-176 pounds), and resem- bled the wolves of Russia and Canada. Wolves are believed to be the ancestor of dogs. All members of the dog family (wolf, dog, coyote, and jackal) are cross-fertile and can form different cross breeds so that there are now dogs of many sizes and breeds. Wolves are thought to be the first animals to form a bond with humans.

About the Author

Henry Shykoff, now retired from a distinguished career in Anaesthesia and Clinical Research, lives in Toronto with his wife Ruth, also a retired physician. Henry is known by family and neighbours as a handyman--a Mr. Fix-it--at their cottage near Peterborough and at home in East York. He is a much-loved storytelling "zeidy" to his grandchildren and a source of useful information to several youngsters to whom he is an honourary grandfather.

This is Henry Shykoff's first book.

Author's Sketch Map of the Area

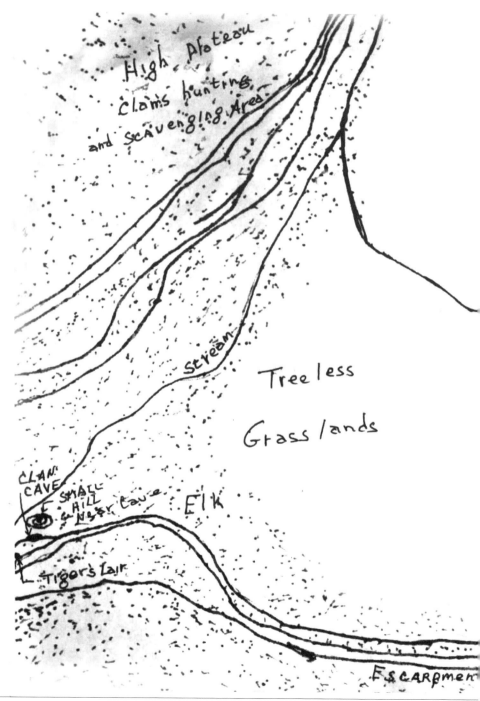

High Plateau
Clan's hunting
and Scavenging Area

stream

Treeless

Grass lands

CLAN CAVE
SMALL HILL
Near Cave
Elk

Tiger's Lair

ESCARPMENT

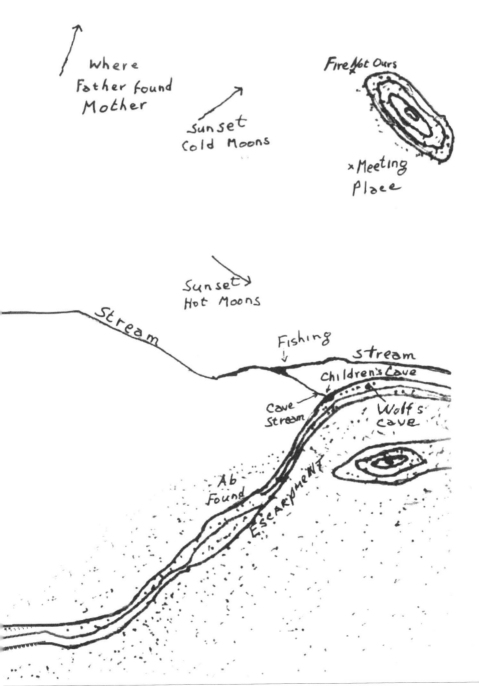